Max Glebow   Brig

Fire Density

Prologue

"Kay, what's up with the signal?" The Lieutenant gave a question that was of interest to everyone.

Shefferson has already been fiddling silently for two minutes with the direction-finder which he took out of his backpack, but, to all appearances, he hasn't yet managed to achieve significant results worthy to be reported to his commander.

"I'm not getting anywhere. The quargs produce jamming, and their interference generator is not so far away, so they are blocking everything completely. With this much counteraction, we'll hear the beacon at a distance of 500 meters at the best."

The dropship made its turbines howl while pulling slowly from the ground and flew to the east above the hills towards the territory controlled by our troops. The plan was for it to find a safe place and wait for us to signal, and if there's no signal within six hours, it has to arrive at a predetermined rendezvous point.

However, it didn't work out. A bright flare and a noisy explosion right behind the hills, just 300 meters away informed us unequivocally that we no longer had transport to return to the base.

"Let's go! Quick! " The Lieutenant jumped up and and giving us an example ran to the nearest gorge between the sandy hills covered with burnt grass. Here and there hills were replaced by barkhans, the desert lay very close by.

Sergeant Ivan Kelt, deputy commander and our pathfinder, went ahead on the watch. I and the second universal commando, Private Gnezdoff, became flank security guards, and now we made our way almost along the top of the hills, trying to keep our heads down while carefully lifting the sensors of scanners just above the ridge. So far, no one's been bothering us, but the tension has literally been in the air. The presence of the enemy was felt almost physically.

For half an hour we've been moving like this, trying to get away from the dropship crash site, and at the same time crossing the search area almost in the middle. The sense of imminent danger had eased slightly, and the Lieutenant gave the squad the signal to stop.

"Kay, let out your dragonflies, 'cause we walk like we're blind. It won't take long to run into quargs."

Shefferson pulled three small cylinder containers from the backpack, pressed the ends slightly in certain places, and dropped them into the air one by one. Containers turned out to be compact unmanned aerial vehicles. They unfolded like baby transformer toys, easily spread their thin wings and were hovering over the squad while quietly buzzing. Shefferson operated them with his helmet, at least I saw no special device in his hands.

The dragonflies flew in three directions, straight ahead and to the right and left at 45 degrees. We kept going, but almost immediately Kay stopped us. One of the dragonflies came across the remains of the scouts' fly-car hit by quargs.

We didn't move to the fly-car crash site. There was a high probability of an ambush there. Lieutenant with Shefferson went over the dragonfly camera footage. The information was distressing. The bodies of the four scouts lay not far from the wreckage of a smoking vehicle like broken dolls. There were eight guys who went out on a mission, which means there were at best four survivors. That is, if no one was left inside the demolished fly-car or died before. But the beacon didn't work from here, or the dragonfly would have picked up it's signal. So someone managed to get away from the crash site. If only we knew in which direction.

The scanner built into my outfit was ringing the alarm. I've adjusted the different tone of the alert to different types of potential hazards and now, without even looking at the information appearing before my eyes, I already knew it was a quarg small recon drone. Single shot of my automatic gun echoed loud down the ravine and the wreckage of a small flying machine swept the hillsides. But we were undeniably discovered, and now the group is going to be hunted down and we haven't even found any surviving scouts yet.

"Anton, you go a hundred meters down the ravine and stay here. Take the enemy away northeast. Go to the rendezvous point yourself, " the Lieutenant assigned task to the universal commando Gnezdoff. "The rest follow me."

"The dragonfly that came to the site of the fly-car's fall is lost," reported Shefferson. "Where to redirect the others, Commander?"

"Let's have them look west. That's where we're going."

"Got it. Doin' it."

Still, there's a reason I spent a couple of days poking around with scanners and EW stations in the Academy tech area. And our tech Jeff was a big help. Results were not long in coming.

"Lieutenant, Sir, I'm picking up a beacon signal. Giving you the bearing."

"Kay, can you confirm the Cadet's information?" the Lieutenant turned to the regular communication specialist.

"Not yet, Commander. My direction-finder is silent."

"We're changing course. Ivan, take to the right, 15."

"Yes, Sir."

We went up a little higher and forward 40 meters.

"There's a signal," Shefferson reported with mistrustful surprise. "Cadet, what kind of scanner do you have in your gear?"

"Standard infantry scanner. But I've adjusted it a bit, and I've got a good tech, he helped me."

"You've got a tech? What rank is he in?"

"A week ago he was a warrant officer. Now he is Lieutenant."

"The warrant officer was given the rank of lieutenant? No school?"

"Put aside that blether," the Lieutenant's raised his voice on us.

"Yes, Sir," Kay and I answered together.

We arrived at the beacon about 20 minutes later. It took us a while to find it. The beacon operated in short pulse mode at floating frequency. To hear it and to take its bearings, you had to know exactly what you were looking for. But again, the lack of a fixed signal made it difficult to find the beacon.

There were two scouts, a sergeant and a corporal, the latter was seriously injured when their fly-car fell. In the same time, he could really walk - exoskeleton is good for that.

"All right, so, fighters," the Lieutenant called the scouts, "we found you, but we don't know what's next. We have no transport, our dropship has been knocked down by quargs. There's almost 400 kilometers in no man's land from here to where we can signal our forces, and, more importantly, where they can safely retrieve us. There's been a lot of quargs running around lately. Did you turn them on?"

"That's right, Lieutenant, Sir," said the Sergeant who introduced himself as Kimi Nukanen, "we went to their control zone and found a heavy robot deployment. Those were Mammoths of the latest model. No less than two divisions. It was in the middle of nowhere. Can you imagine how happy the command of our forces on Kapteen would be? That almost certainly means preparing for a ground offensive. And we, the naive ones, were waiting to be struck from space. Well, we were spotted on the exit. The quargs certainly did not wish to let such information leak. At first we got away, but we lost two of our own. We came at the fly-car's rendezvous point. You probably know the rest."

"We know," the Lieutenant nodded his head in agreement and started thinking. The subordinates waited silently for the commander's decision.

"We go to the rendezvous point. Anton should be waiting for us there. The dropship, of course, will not come, but when we're not back in time, they'll send a drone. If we're lucky, it'll pick up and record our signal. If it can return to base after that, they'll send a dropship, after us. Any questions?"

There were no questions.

"Then let the wounded go into the center of the column. Ivan - to the main patrol, Lavroff and Nukanen - to the sides. John, keep an eye on the rear. Kay, call off one of the dragonflies, we should save energy. For how long we'll be here, no one knows. Go. "

Private Anton Gnezdoff never made it to the rendezvous point. Not the first day, nor the second. The drone did come, circled the dot, automatically responded that the signal had been received, and turned into a flash of bright flame from the impact of an enemy missile. And five minutes later, we were pinned down tight by a heavy infantry squad and a Small Dragon. Well, it looked like it was my turn to act.

We slowly retreated under the squeal of the shards and the roar of the Dragon's automatic cannon constantly shooting our way out from every safe haven.

"Cadet, are you ready?" From the sound of the Lieutenant's voice, there was doubt. He has already lost one universal commando, but Alexey was sure of Gnezdoff, and that guy must have done his job at the cost of his life. The Lieutenant didn't know much about me, but he didn't have any other options anyway.

"That's right, Lieutenant, Sir. Which way to draw the enemy?"

"First, hold them here. Then lead around the rendezvous point. Give us an hour's head start and leave. We're gonna go east. We'll try to get out on foot. We'll turn on the beacon every four hours for ten minutes for you."

"I got it. I'm ready."

"Good luck, Cadet. And thank you for the missile brought down. Well done."

"Serving…"

"Put it aside, Lavroff. Squadron, follow me in the usual way. Go!"

And I was left alone.

The quargs didn't get ahead. Either they were waiting for reinforcements or they weren't feeling very confident, although their superiority of firepower was noticeable, even when our unit hasn't split up yet. Now I had to play the whole group by myself.

Basically, with my equipment, I didn't see anything impossible about it. My possession of three kinds of weapons made it possible to simulate different activities. That's what I've been doing since I activated the second EW station in my spacesuit. This mode absorbed a lot of energy, but it's become much harder to detect me with standard scanners. The Leiten-5 experience was very useful.

I fired three rounds from my automatic gun at the robot that stuck itself out in the open. I didn't manage to penetrate it's armor, but I spoiled his mood and forced him to hide behind a massive rock. Now it was time to change positions and wait a little bit, keeping my head down. My scanner picked up some questionable activity at the top of the hill, and I fired in a burst from the rotary machine gun on its crest without trying to hit anyone, but simply showing the enemy the presence of a shooter with a different weapon. Right after that, I stepped back and started to pick a position to work with a sniper rifle. The caliber of this rifle was, by the way, 18 millimeters, so only the Small Dragon pilot could feel relatively secure.

The alarmingly screeching scanner informed me that the quargs had launched a drone in my direction. They wanted to know where the shooters were, which was understandable. The drone was a small machine that didn't fly fast, though it tried to hide in the folds of the area, briefly showing up from behind the rocks and the crests of the hills. It was almost a perfect target for a sniper rifle, especially if it was guided not by a man, but by computer-aided fire control. Shot, and the drone, which was broken through, fell to the ground as a pile of useless junk, but my position it marked and managed to transmit the information. The Small Dragon did not spare me a rocket, which was primarily intended to fire at air targets, but with a manual guidance, it was quite suitable for destroying enemies on the ground. My light armor was highly contraindicated to take direct hits or be in the vicinity of explosions of something heavy. So I jumped aside, made a roll and one more jump to the big rock, which took the brunt of the strike elements. I changed position once again...

I knew the quargs would soon get bored of this dance, and they would try to outflank the evil shooters. Except they're not the only ones who can use drones, I love and respect these machines, too. On Leiten-5 I liked very much the black 'cockroaches' of Captain Mbia, and I cadged three pieces from him. Little arthropod devices the size of mice have sprung up to the top of the nearest hills. Within line-of-sight range they were communicating with my suit through laser-optical channels and ignored virtually any interference. But now I saw what was going on in the back slopes of the nearest heights. I had a flying drone, too, but only one, and I decided to save it for the time being.

And in the back slopes, there was something interesting going on. Two quargs in heavy infantry armour moved gently along the ridge of the nearest hill, bypassing me on my right. There were another two on the left, and in front of me, distracting my attention, the combat robot was constantly bustling around, it kept popping out of hiding and shooting at me. The Small Dragon pilot wasn't afraid of my gun, because from that distance it could only scratch the paint on his armor, well, maybe leave some small dents. Well, that was not a luxury fly-car. Scars like that are true decorations for a war machine.

There was an urgent need to resolve the problem of this bypass. Having fired my gun at random, not to hit someone or make the quargs hide, but to show them that I'm here and I'm not gone, I moved back and left. I moved pretty hard so I could get in the way of the couple of enemies that tried to bypass me, but keep out of their sight. I wasn't going to kill them, I had another job to do. I need to slow down my pursuers, so I'll hold them back. The bullet from a sniper rifle of my caliber, when hit in the limb, causes a serious wound, even if the enemy is in a heavy infantry space suit. After the shooting, I hid immediately, and watched the result with the help of the 'cockroach'.

The result met my expectations. The unharmed quarg tried to pull the wounded from the battlefield, constantly staring and at any second expecting a new bullet from the invisible sniper. But the sniper kept quiet. I still didn't shoot when the aggrieved couple got help from two more infantrymen under the cover of that Small Dragon with the slightly scratched paint on the armor. I was wondering where they were taking the wounded. They arrived here by something.

Using some specialized device, the quargs quickly placed the injured on the back of the robot, and the machine ran over the hill without losing any time. My 'cockroaches' could not see that far, so I decided to risk the flying drone. I gave the miniature flyer an order to escort the robot, ordering it to keep a max distance from the target.

In the absence of the robot, the enemy infantry did not attack and kept quiet. I knew it wasn't for long. I didn't think they had their dropship far away, because they came at us pretty fast after our drone reached the rendezvous point. So I used the pause to break off the enemy and to get to the rendezvous point that I'd assigned to my flying scout.

The quarg dropship was within fifteen minutes of a careful and slow march. My opponents lost me and now they were probably trying to figure out where I got to, and where the main group went. According to my orders, I've been truthfully dragging the quargs up and down the hills for an hour. I was supposed to get back to the squadron, but it wasn't my plan, at least now. I knew perfectly well that if I left now, I'd be at a dead end again. The power in the suit accumulators will soon be depleted. It wouldn't gonna be enough for a 400-kilometer walk in the desert. So, what's next? To try to get out on foot, unarmed, and in just overalls? No. It's better to risk doing something now.

I got to the dropship when the quargs were still shaking the hills and ravines in search of the missing enemy scouts. The robot ran to the aid of its infantry a long time ago, leaving the wounded in the care of the pilot and another quarg in the armor, who was assigned to the dropship apparently for security. Now the pilot was fiddling with the suit of the wounded quarg lying on the dropped ramp of the ship, and the guard was standing there, looking around.

Two dry clicks of my sniper rifle shots scattered across the hilly plain. The enemies sank down on the ground like weak puppets, but the signal of the attack on the dropship must have gone to the main group of quargs. Of course, I was hoping that my jammer wouldn't let that signal get through, but the distance from which I fired did not let me be entirely certain, especially considering the fact that my position was not between the dropship and the main enemy forces, but on the side, otherwise I just wouldn't see the target.

I ran without saving energy and squeezing maximum speed out of my gear. Every second could have been crucial. I didn't kill the wounded quarg, just shoved him off the ramp with the pilot's body and dived into the shadowy insides of the quarg dropship. I almost fell over a body in a space suit. That was a human space suite. Anton Gnezdoff was lying on the side of the ship and showed no sign of life. I saw a ragged hole in the chest plate of his armor, it looked like he was hit by a large shard. But the private was alive although unconscious. I couldn't afford to look into his condition now and jumped further to the cockpit.

With the completion of operation at Leiten-5, I had quite a lot of time on my way back to Ganymede. Jeff and I had something to do. Remembering my adventures in a terribly uncomfortable quarg tech's suit, I decided to throw away everything that had nothing to do with hacking enemy machines out of this suit. We mercilessly dismantled the armor, the weapons, the positioning and sighting system, the scanners and even the exoskeleton itself. So, as a result, it turned out to be a pretty compact device, which, if you wanted to, could be easily installed inside our human, heavy infantry space suit. And, of course, as I gathered up my equipment for this trip, I hadn't forgotten about this device. The challenge was something else. I've never tried to hack a flying quarg machine, and all my knowledge of it was theoretical. But there was no other way, especially in light of the discovery of wounded Anton in the dropship.

I activated the equipment. Lucky for me, the dropship didn't hide any surprises compared to combat robots. It was protected far worse than the Mammoths and even the Small Dragons, so, eight minutes later, I had the enemy machine in my hands. Except I've never flown one of these before. In a previous life, I did well piloting a small troop transport Cuirassier, in this life I piloted our dropship. But I've never had a quarg flying machine in my hands before. It was required to take immediate action, so I plunged without doubt into a mad picture, which the enemy vehicle's targeting and navigation system projected on my helmet's visor. For taking off like this, our pilot instructor would have killed me if I were there, then he'd bring me back to life by means of a mighty kick in the ass and would kill me again. He would repeat the procedure until the necessary pedagogical effect was achieved.

The dropship was wobbling from side to side. I almost hit the nearest hill but only slightly grazed it and raised a cloud of sand. Nevertheless, I was flying. It was a good thing no one's tried to shoot me yet. The machine I was flying was an easy target now.

At first I just flew away. Having realized that I can already, somehow or other, manage horizontal flight and careful maneuvering, I turned my attention to weapons. There were no thermobaric rocket launching containers that are so dear to the heart of any human commando. Instead, quargs suspended under one of the short wings an additional high-speed aircraft gun, and under the other wing - an air-to-air missile launcher with a laser-optical guidance system, which is used to follow the target manually. Looked like that was who shot on our planes and the dropship. Judging by the amount of missiles used up, I'd say it was so. The quargs knew we'd send a rescue team for the scouts. They flew in early, picked up a position, disguised the dropship, turned on the EW station, and quietly waited for guests. It was a perfectly sensible decision. But an evil brigadier general showed up and ruined the party. At least, let's hope so.

I was no longer interested in the group of quargs running around the hills. I remembered there was still one missile left in the Small Dragon's backpack, and at my level of piloting, meeting that missile didn't seem like a good idea. I bypassed the threatened area along a wide arc, pressing the dropship belly against the hills, and even sometimes diving into the most spacious gorges. By my calculations, I've already beat Lieutenant Egorov's team by ten kilometers. I didn't risk arriving to them on an enemy dropship. They could just begin shooting before they can figure it out. Having landed the capricious machine in a small hollow, I went to the landing bay and squatted down in front of Anton. The quargs didn't deactivate his suit. That's all that kept the Private alive. The embedded first aid kit was doing what it could, but its prognosis was getting more and more threatening. If Gnezdoff isn't in the hospital within the next five hours, there's no way to save him. Which means we probably won't have time to land in our control zone and call for help. I'm gonna have to brazenly fly the enemy machine right onto the runway of the special forces' base. I don't think I'd be welcome...

I caught the beacon signal two hours later. I couldn't waste time any more, so I took the dropship in the air.

***

A group that had already lost two people was moving east pretty vigorously. But it was OK just for now. There was still power left in the accumulators for another five hours. Lieutenant Egorov's mood was getting worse by the minute. He didn't see a real way out and led the group forward out of sheer stubbornness. Kay Shefferson raised his hand, urging the group to stop.

"Commander, I've picked up a drone, a human one. But this is not my dragonfly, it's something else."

Soon they saw the device. It slowly approached, circled the group with a slight buzzing and withdrew behind the ridge of the nearest hill.

"John, look what it is," ordered Alexey.

The sniper went up the hill, raised an optical scanner over its ridge, and then he went straight down to the squad.

"There's a quarg dropship, Commander. It's on the ground, the ramp is open, and near it stands our Cadet in his 'barn' with guns. He waved at me."

"Are you not overheated, John? Send me the file."

When the Lieutenant started playing it, he looked for a few seconds into the image projected onto the helmet visor, then silently slapped the sniper on the shoulder, made a sign to the subordinates to follow and climbed the hill.

***

Major Weber was pulled from the table by the howl of an air-raid warning.

"Duty Officer, report!" ordered the Major via communicator.

"An enemy dropship has entered the control zone."

"Alone? No cover?"

"That's right. Altitude is one kilometer. It flies slowly. Doesn't maneuver. It makes an ideal target."

"Wait, Lieutenant. Something's wrong here. I've never noticed quarg suicidal tendencies before."

"It could be a diversion, or it could be a simulator."

"Put the battalion on combat alert. Make air defence equipment fully operational. The dropship can launch missiles from ten kilometers. How far is it now?"

"105. If it doesn't change speed, it'll enter the firing range in fifteen minutes."

"Call the interceptors."

"Yes, Sir!... Major, Sir! There's a signal from the dropship! It's unstable yet. I can't make it out. But the coding is ours."

"What the hell…? Turn it on me."

The Major's office was filled with cracking noise through which sometimes incoherent pieces of words burst. But with each passing minute, the distance decreased and the quality of the communication improved.

"…ship calls… ..ber Dropship … Major Weber. …tenant Egorov's group returns from mis… Pri… seriously wounded. Request emergency evacuation to hospi…"

"Scheißer! Don't shoot!" shouted the Major via communicator. "Call back the interceptors! Get medics and emergency crew on the runway right away."

***

"Major, Sir, have you sent Cadet Lavroff back to Academy?"

"Yes, I have, Lieutenant. He earned the low-level combat experience he needed in one mission abundantly. His practice ended there, so the Cadet left. And he took the dropship with him as a legal trophy. I didn't mind."

"That's a pity, I had no time to talk to him. You have introduced me to the promotion. I'd be happy to give him my group, with a completely calm conscience. When he finishes his studies, naturally."

"You're still a rookie, Lieutenant," Webber laughed so hard, "Haven't you read his file?"

"At first, there was no time," Lieutenant was embarrassed, "And then there was no need. It just became clear what a man was worth."

"Would you at least look out of curiosity," squeezed the Major out of laughter, "Who did you want to offer the group to? This Cadet of yours had been commanding a Heavy Commando Brigade for a month on the quargs-occupied Leiten-5. Generals are certainly waiting for him to graduate from the Academy, the Generals with such shoulder straps that you and I are very far away. Well, Lieutenant. It's been a long time since I've had this much fun."

Chapter 1

The front didn't collapse, but it cracked quite a bit. As it turned out later, this was the first, but very bad, wake-up call that marked a difficult time for people. A distracting quarg strike on Leiten star system caused the Earth Federation to react sharply, and draw on significant reserves to address the threat. As a result, it was almost impossible to counterbalance a strong and unexpected blow in the other direction - it was an attack on the Federation planets of stars Gliese-338 and Grumbridge-

1618. This led to a serious defence crisis, which the people were unable to overcome quickly.

When I returned to the Academy, the high command was in a very nervous state. Reserves have been raked out wherever it's been possible, and Lieutenant General Shiller had to reluctantly agree to the early graduation of third-year cadets. As it happens in such cases those cadets received only one star on their shoulder straps instead of two and the rank of second lieutenant, which was rare in the army. Suddenly I was out of the job as an instructor, since it was the graduate course of the Academy that mastered the captured machines.

Academy director called me back to his office. When I tried to report, he waved it away annoyingly and silently pointed me to the meeting table.

"Cadet Lavroff, " began gloomily the General, whose mood fluctuated at the mark 'below the skirting board', "you've certainly done a great job, and you are a hero. Colonel Kreps sent me Major Weber's report on your practice. For your rescue mission, he recommended you for the Iron Cross. We, Germans, prefer to recommend deserving soldiers for precisely this award." A light shadow of smile appeared on the General's gloomy face. "Kreps approved the recommendation, punch a hole in the tunic."

"Serving the Earth Federation."

"Ehh, yes. And you serve it pretty good. Except with the situation on the front... Do you know, Lavroff, when was the last time we had to throw undertrained cadets into battle?" Forced to sign the order for the early graduation of the third course the General couldn't calm down.

"That was in the first year of the was with quargs, General, Sir."

"That's it. Twenty years ago. Do you understand where we have returned?"

"These are temporary difficulties caused by the strategic error and intelligence deficiencies. We shall undoubtedly prevail, Gen... "

"Put ranks aside, Cadet. "

"Yes, Sir."

"You're right! The recon guys have overslept, to put it mildly, preparations for strikes on Gliese and Grumbridge. And right you are about Leiten system - too much force was thrown in there, although this mistake may have saved the lives of you personally and of our freshmen."

"Not of all of them, unfortunately."

"Not of all of them. This is war, Cadet, you know it as good as me, or better yet, I haven't been in a fight in a while.

And that's the second question I want to discuss with you. We've already lost almost half our freshmen and we've lost the opportunity to prepare well our graduates. I wouldn't be surprised if they cut the curriculum down to two years. Now freshmen, your comrades, are better prepared for battle than sophomore cadets, and, probably better than those fresh second lieutenants who have just been graduates. I need practical advice based on your combat experience. I have to turn the remaining cadets into officers who will not be killed in the first battle with their units. Don't look at me with wild eyes. Yes, the General asks the Cadet to share his combat experience. Have you recently looked in the mirror at your qualification tab?"

"I can tell you one thing, if it wasn't for the six months we spent at the Academy, none of us would have come back from Leiten-5. When our ship was hit by several shells and began to drift uncontrollably towards the planet, the cadets remained a capable military formation despite the deaths of the officers. The platoon commanders did not lose control of their subordinates, and as a result, the landing took place with minimal casualties. You've prepared us well, Lieutenant General, Sir. What we had frankly missed was heavy weaponry and experience of guerrilla activities and sabotage. If it wasn't for Captain Mbia's men, I don't know how we'd get away with it. I'm afraid that in the new circumstances commandos will be regularly caught in such situations of complete encirclement and isolation from the main forces. We need knowledge in this sphere and reconnaissance equipment. I've been meaning to report my proposals to establish a special recon platoon equipped as regular scouts in each commando battalion, but since you called me yourself, I'd like to take this opportunity."

"Usually, scouts are assigned to commandos at the time of landing, if the command deems it necessary. Your case was special. No one was planning on sending you into battle, so you had to work it out on your own. I do not yet see arguments in favor of a special platoon in each battalion."

"You told us yourself that a saboteur and a commando are different military specialties. From Captain Mbia's men, I'm very well aware of that. They're good scouts, but they're not first line fighters. They can't be sent to attack. They just don't have the training and equipment for this kind of battle, and I was desperately short of men on Leiten-5 who could attack in the regimental order of battle, and then, if necessary, become saboteurs. Everyone in the landing party has to fight. This rule has been known since pre-Cosmic times," here again it's been far-fetched from the experience of my past life.

"Well, that makes sense," said the General after a moment of reflection. "Prepare a report, Cadet, I'll review it, and maybe I'll give it a go. And now I have news for you. Yesterday at the Academy's board of trustees meeting we talked about you. The Chairman of the Council, General of the Army Vasnetsov joked that we have cadets in the Academy with sufficient combat experience to enter the General Staff Academy. Laugh all you want, but after the meeting I pulled your file. You're a ready candidate for the Academy. You've had enough experience in command positions. The only thing you need is a higher military education, and only officers are allowed in the Academy. You're 16 now, as strange as it sounds. I keep getting the feeling that I'm dealing with someone my own age, but from a formal point of view, it doesn't change the case. You've done enough for the Academy to make its director in my person want to take part in your destiny," grinned the General, "but the only person in the Earth Federation who can authorize officer promotion circumventing the age limit is the President. I've spoken to Vasnetsov, and he's ready to make a presentation to the President for you to be promoted to the rank of second lieutenant. I'll sign the recommendation, too. We need the signatures of three other high-ranking officers who know you personally and can vouch for you. Do you have an idea?"

"Colonel General Knyazev, Admiral Nelson, Admiral Fulton," without hesitation I listed,"I really don't know Admiral Nelson personally, but he commanded the operation to free Leiten-5, and I think the Colonel General can persuade him to sign this document."

"You didn't waste any time," grinned the General, "Fulton and Knyazev can't stand each other. To the extent that this is known well beyond the Fifth Strike Fleet. If you manage to collect both these signatures on the same document...Okay, enough of this stuff. Let's start, perhaps, with Knyazev."

***

We fought off the quarg attack at the cost of losing the Gliese-338 system and almost complete destruction of the infrastructure in Grumbridge-1618, but the enemy's advance was stopped. The early graduates were even sent back to the Academy to finish their studies. A little over a quarter of those who left the Planetary Commando Academy 40 days ago have returned.

For the next four months, I worked like wood-carver Geppetto on the Pinocchios' assembly line. The director of the Academy had drawn up a plan for me to crash into my wretched head and the motor centers of the spinal cord the knowledge of all specialized subjects for which the cadets were normally given two and a half years of learning. I was handling it, but I sank into bed in the evening like a sack of potatoes and fell into a dead sleep until the morning. And then I was called to the capital, to Earth, to be awarded the Gold Star.

I didn't like the situation on the front lines. When I came here, the balance of opposing forces seemed steady, and I thought I had at least five years left to get promoted and to make useful connections and improve my abilities. Now I realized clearly that if I wouldn't act now, The Earth Federation risked losing the war before I can complete my mission. It was time to put a team together. I wouldn't manage to do this alone.

Once again, as the first day of my life in this world, I decided to analyze my assets and liabilities. The task of constructing the portal gates so far was as unattainable as when I arrived at the hospital on Titan. I saw no direct and quick way to solve it. Well, let's take advantage of the way that's as old as the world, and divide a big problem into a lot of little pieces. I need the knowledge, resources, people and permission of the authorities to build and test the gate. I have the knowledge. But it's not exactly the kind of knowledge I need. I won't build the gate myself, which means the information in my head needs to be legitimized. How to do that? The cadet and even the second lieutenant, if the response to the submission is positive, don't have that kind of knowledge. So what we need is an official organization that can present this information as its own development. That's number one.

Now regarding the resourses. At the moment it's primarily money. Right now, my personal account contains just over 32,000,000 federal rubles. These are patent royalties, instructor's wages, trophy prizes and gratuities attached to the Iron Cross and Gold Star. That seems to be quite a lot. With this money, one can comfortably live in the capital of the Federation for almost ten years. But it concerns a common man. I'm a person who's very restless and unprepared to just sit on his ass, so this money will be enough only for a start. So, the question of resources is soon to be resolved, but not right now. That's number two. Next on my list are people. I'm supposed to pursue a career in the army where I'm not even an officer yet. So, all the current affairs of providing resources and the activities of the company yet to be created will have to be handled by someone else. I mean, sure, I'm gonna go for it, but I might not have the time or the opportunity. I started thinking and almost immediately remembered Lieutenant Jeff, my senior technician. He should be interviewed one of the first. Professor Stein of The Colonial Technological Institute may also be of use. His name and connections will certainly prove useful. And I need to talk to Inga. I could really use a trusted person at the company. To be honest, I really wanted her to give up her military career, but knowing her, I was kind of afraid to even talk about it.

So, basically, the plan has been ready. First, a weapons development firm. It'll help me solve two problems at once. I will slowly feed my knowledge from the past life into it and embed it into new weapons samples, thereby legalizing the information I need. And money, of course. The development of the gate will require just an enormous amount of money, which the Federation treasury would never give me, and that way I'll spend the company's profits. The second, no less important than the first, is the military career. By the time the gate is built, I must have sufficient influence in the authorities to provide the contact of civilizations according to my scenario. And third, it's time to help the Federation with new technologies, otherwise we may not live to fulfill that contact.

***

The capital of the Earth Federation, the huge city of Amundsen, is located at the south pole of the planet, in the heart of Antarctica, covered with forests. In the middle of the twenty-first century, the human race here finally succeeded in contaminating the home planet, with irreversible environmental consequences. Waste islands in the oceans, man-made disasters on oil platforms and chemical plants, oxidation of ocean waters with carbon dioxide, filling the atmosphere with dust and its poisoning combined with the increasing overpopulation of the planet, all of this has led to people barely surviving to develop terraforming technologies. And the first planet to which terraforming had to be applied was the Earth itself.

An artificial thermonuclear sun hung above the south pole, melting the ice and giving to the suffocating and thirsty mankind source of fresh water and oxygen extracted from it. This seemed to be a temporary solution, but it allowed people to survive to the point where the deep purification plants built along the air and sea currents would bring the concentration of harmful substances in the atmosphere and oceans to an acceptable level. Humanity no longer made such mistakes, and the environmental protection began to be treated on the Earth with blatant fanaticism. Not surprisingly, the ice-free southern continent has become a forest- and lake-covered paradise, in the middle of which humanity, grateful for its salvation, has jointly built an ecologically exemplary mega-city which became the capital of the Federation.

There was a spring in the southern hemisphere of the Earth, and the Antarctic sun also imitated this pleasant season. The awards ceremony was two days away, and since I was in the capital, I decided to take care of my future corporation. I didn't know much about local law, so I went to a small consulting firm I found online, whose pages seemed adequate to me.

"Good afternoon, I am the leading lawyer of 'JurTex' Leo Rabinovich," the man who answered my call was a vibrant man in his 30s, "What can our company do for you?"

"Igor Lavroff," I said in return, "I need to register a company that will be able to take part in the State procurement competition."

"Sphere of activity?"

"Development and supply of weapons and military equipment."

Rabinovich had a glimpse of surprise, but he kept on talking calmly:

"This activity requires State licensing. The list of requirements for obtaining a licence is extensive. There is a need for a production base, qualified staff, minimum registered capital requirements."

"That's why I asked for your advice."

"Tell me, Igor, do you plan to become the founder and owner of the company?"

"No. I'm a minor. My mother will own the company."

"How much are you planning to invest in the capital of the new organization?"

"30,000,000 rubles."

Rabinovich didn't give a damn. None of his business where a 16-year-old boy took that money. Maybe he's the son of a wealthy businessman, maybe it's an inheritance. Who cares?

"Well, that's enough, at least, to comply with the law. I can take your case, but to obtain a license for such an activity I need from you a number of documents, which confirm that you have experience in the development of new weapons, as well as the results of tests of your products and recommendations from high-ranking military officers. Are you able to provide them?" in the eyes of the lawyer there was doubt.

"I think so. But it's gonna take some time."

"Then we can do this: I'll register a company for you. This will be the first stage of our cooperation, a rather inexpensive one. Next, as you provide the necessary documents, we will proceed to obtain a license. Here, prepare the money, Igor. It will not cost you less than half a million rubles."

***

The rewarding ceremony was very solemn. 35 persons to be awarded were assembled in the main column hall. The award was broadcast online throughout the Federation. In addition to the President, there were many high-ranking officials and military officers. I was licking my lips in anticipation while looking at this flower garden of potentialities, but my insignificant rank has isolated me from them as well as thick tank armor. Earth Federation President, Marshal Ivan Tobolsky, 60-year-old impressionable man with a thick mane of gray hair, a nose with a light hump, a strong chin and piercing brown eyes, delivered a speech that was traditional for such cases, but was slightly adapted to the current situation on the fronts, which was by no means the best. Therefore, we've heard repeatedly: «in this difficult time», «it is time for hard tests» and «verification of our will to win». And then he went straight to the award. A tall and smooth general who summoned my association with the word 'parquet' gave the name of the next recipient, and the guy in question approached the President with a report while marching in a ceremonial pace. Most of the time Tobolsky smiled habitually, took the award from a tray his extremely solemn assistant was holding, handed it to the hero and shook his hand with congratulations. The decorated man responded with a statutory phrase and returned to the line. Sometimes the President spoke to the officer or soldier a few words in a quiet voice and even listened to the answer. It was impossible to understand exactly what they were saying.

I turned out to be one of the last.

"Commander in Chief, Sir, Cadet of the Planetary Commando Academy Igor Lavroff has arrived for the state award!" I reported clearly to the President.

"Leiten-5? Commanding the Heavy Commando Brigade and striking to meet our landing party?" suddenly asked Tobolsky. There was a glimpse of surprise on the face of the foppish general who heard the question.

"That's right, Commander in Chief, Sir."

"Congratulations on the Order of the Gold Star, Second Lieutenant. And on joining the General Staff Academy. Now more than ever, we need such commanders."

"Serving the Earth Federation," I answered according the regulations, standing at attention.

"Unique Specialist?" The President quietly asked, nodding at the badge on my tunic and having thrown the ceremonial General into final shock by deviating from protocol. "Do you have any requests or suggestions?"

I, too, was barely keeping my face cool, but I wasn't going to miss an opportunity like this.

"That's right, Commander in Chief, Sir. I do."

"After the ceremony wait for my assistant. And now you're free to go, Second Lieutenant."

There was no miracle, no personal meeting with the President, but his assistant did find me after the awards ceremony, and diligently concealing his disdain for a person as insignificant as a second lieutenant, invited me to submit my requests and views in writing and send it to him for processing and transmission to the Commander in Chief.

***

The door to the President's office opened silently and the well trained assistant brought the Head of State coffee and ginger cookies. Tobolsky silently nodded.

"Mr. President, you asked me to remind you of Second Lieutenant Lavroff."

"Ah, Lavroff. Yes, thank you," - Tobolsky wearily moved his hand along his face. "What's there? Just briefly."

"He claims that in the operations on Leiten-5 and Kapteen, he used weapon systems of his own design, based on our and trophy circuitry and built on the Academy tech base and in the field conditions. According to him, they were far more effective in combat than our standard models."

"Did you check that?"

"Yes, Mr. President, I've sent inquiries to his commanding officers. The answers have been strictly positive. In the case of Leiten-5, there is even a specific combat efficiency calculation: 130 percent."

"Hmm. Let's say it's OK. What does he want? Money for development or transfer to a defense industrial complex?"

"Oddly enough, no. He doesn't ask for money and only sees himself in combat units. He requests a licence to develop arms and military equipment for a company he has just registered as well as unhindered access to the Ministry of Defence competitions."

"What's the problem with the license?"

"It has been the practice of the Ministry of Defence to issue such licences only to large enterprises within the defence industry complex and to their subsidiaries. There's no way for a small firm just set up to get a license like this. They just won't let you, even after fulfilling the formal requirements. I mean, there's so many of them, you can always pick on something."

"Let's not get in his way. This guy might be useful to us. Someone in the Military Industrial Complex has overdone things, and this guy, if he doesn't turn out to be nothing, which I don't think he will be, could be a good pain in the ass... What is required of me?"

"Recommending a license with your signature will solve all the problems."

"Is draft paper ready?"

"Yes, Mr. President."

"Send it to me, I'll sign it. And let me know if he makes any sense."

***

Leo Rabinovich froze up, staring at the screen of his tablet. I understood him well. I sat like that yesterday, stupidly reading and rereading the recommendation to issue the Lavroff Weapons Company a license to develop arms and military equipment, signed personally by President Tobolsky.

Finally, the lawyer stopped scrutinizing the document and gave me a still slightly stunned look.

"I think, Igor, in a week you'll be licensed. With such a recommendation, it is unlikely that anyone would pay attention to formalities, because, in fact, Mr President himself has assumed full responsibility. You've earned a lot of trust, though."

I just hemmed vaguely. I didn't expect it myself. And some little worm of doubt was scratching somewhere in my brain, banging hammers into the top of my head: there's no free cheese in rat labyrinths.

"I'm more than happy with the week," I told Rabinovich, "But I have to get started somewhere. Can your company find me an office space and an experimental workshops site?"

"I think so. It won't be a problem. It's not hard to rent an office in the capital, if one has money. It's pretty simple with a production site, but not on Earth, of course. There's no way you're gonna be allowed to set up a production site here, but the Moon is at your complete disposal. There are huge tech parks where they will be happy to rent you out the necessary space, perhaps even together with the equipment."

"Then, Leo, get the list of the parameters of the site and the office that I need, and I'm looking for suggestions."

***

"Good afternoon, Ivan Gerkhardovich," I decided not to delay calling Professor Stein, "Do you have a few minutes for me?"

"Glad to see you, Igor," the professor gave me a sincere smile. Of course, I'm the one he has extremely positive memories with, both emotionally and financially, "Always happy to talk to you. But you didn't just bring up the provincial professor. Surely you have another adventure for me. Am I right?"

"As always, Ivan Gerkhardovich, as always," I didn't deny it, "But I'm also very happy to see you in a good mood."

"Well, tell me, then. Why waste time?"

"I've registered a company and I'm going to develop weapons for our army. In a week's time, I'll have the necessary license, office and space to house the production equipment. I need people, good engineers and scientists to develop EW systems, armor and cannons, and then utilize all this into prototypes of spacesuits, dropships and combat robots. Ten people will be enough for now. I'll send you a list of the skills needed. Could you find me such people among the best students of the Colonial Technological Institute or among recent graduates? I need young people with open-minded brains capable of perceiving and developing breakthrough ideas."

"Give me your list, I'll see what I can do."

I sent the professor a pre-prepared paper. A couple of minutes later, Stein stopped reading and looked up at me.

"I think I will. I see you've already indicated the approximate salary levels. I don't think any of my candidates would give up on that. It'll take me a few days to talk to the right people."

"Thank you, professor, I had no doubt that you could help me recruit people. But that is not all," I said, observing a slight surprise and interest on Stein's face, "To manage this team, I need an experienced leader with the necessary knowledge and authority in the scientific community."

"And you want me to help you find such a man?"

"No, Ivan Gerkhardovich, I don't. I already found him. This man is you. If you want to, of course. But something tells me you're not gonna say no," I smiled rapaciously.

The professor started thinking. He didn't see it coming.

"Hmm," Stein vaguely hemmed, "about another adventure, I did guess. I'd probably send someone else with that idea a long way away. I'm too used to the Colonial Technological Institute, I've got all my roots in it."

"Professor," I told Stein quietly, "do you watch the news regularly?"

"Yes, I do, from time to time."

"And what do you see? Do you think I'd start this whole thing if everything was okay? Why? I'm not poor already.

And as you can see, I'm a soldier, not a scientist. And suddenly, I make this offer. Why do you think?"

The professor looked at me silently.

"When I first met you, I was dying of asteroid fever. And then, to avoid death, I became a scientist for a while. And now I come back to you, and I'm ready to do science and engineering again. I'm dead sick again, Professor. But I'm not the only one sick this time. The whole Federation is sick. And if we don't create a cure right now, we all die. Some will die in space and in the colonies fighting the quargs, and someone in the Solar System under bombs and orbital strikes when there's no one left to protect the planets. There will be no Colonial Technological Institute, no artificial sun over Titan. It's a matter of several years. We need a cure, professor, and this cure is a new weapon. I'll give it to the Federation, with or without you, but I'd rather do it with you."

"Is it that bad?"

"I was there and I saw it with my own eyes."

The professor looked away, and for a while, he was thinking about something of his own. Finally, he looked me in the eye again.

"Where and when do I bring the science and engineering team?"

Chapter 2

I spoke to the newly-made Lieutenant of the Corps of Engineers, Jeff, shortly after the call to the professor. He took my idea calmly, but surprised me with his answer.

"Commander, I'm with you, what's there to talk about? As much new hardware as I've seen and touched in the last few months with you, I've never seen before in my life. And not only did I see it, but I thoughtfully looked into it, and then I tested it in combat. This is a dream, not a service! And something tells me there'll be no problem with such things in your new firm. Just talk to the director of the Academy. I owe him a lot. They wouldn't have made me lieutenant without him. I'm supposed to have taken an individual training course at the Academy. Although why 'supposed', if I'm talking to my instructor now," the Lieutenant smiled, "Yeah, and I wouldn't want to leave the army now, when I've just become an officer."

"All right, Jeff. I'll talk to the Lieutenant General, I think we can find a way that works for everyone, and then I'll contact you again."

Lieutenant General Shiller left me his personal contact, sending me to the capital for an award, so now I could go straight to him.

The director of the Academy didn't respond to the call, but he called back 20 minutes later.

"So, Second Lieutenant, congratulations on the Federation Award, the new rank, and the Staff Academy. Don't stand at attention, the call isn't official. And put aside ranks."

"Thank you for your help. All of this is largely due to you."

"I watched the awards broadcast. What were you talking to the President about for a minute? General Gallo nearly burst on the spot from such a breach of protocol," Shiller grinned.

"That's what I wanted to talk to you about. Please, look at this document," I sent the General a copy of the recommendation signed by President Tobolsky.

"You're such a dodger, Lavroff. How do you get those papers?" a minute later, the general laughed. "First Admiral Petrov, now Mr President himself... You just have the talent to be in the right place at the right time with the right words. And what do you want from me?"

"I need a chief engineer. A talented technician familiar with weapons specifics. You've got one of those."

"I'm not giving Jeff away. So far, everything you've done has been good for the Academy. Now you want to steal my best tech?"

"No, I don't. He wouldn't leave the service himself, much less you."

"What do you want then?" - the General was surprised.

"I want a mutually beneficial partnership with the Planetary Commando Academy. You can send Lieutenant Jeff to my company as a military advisor or just a consultant, after all. At my official invitation, of course. To insure the cooperation of weapons developers with the army and to make certain that the needs of troops are most fully taken into account in the development of new equipment. I need a talented technician. So do you. His qualifications will only increase in my company, and the Academy through him will have access to the latest developments of my company, which are just being tested. And, of course, I'll only have him spending just a part of his time, so he'll be able also to perform his duties at the Academy, albeit in a somewhat reduced form."

"You're not just a dodger, Second Lieutenant," - the general laughed, "You are a Super Dodger. And the invitation to Jeff, I suspect you've already prepared?"

"I'm sending it to you."

***

On May 15th I, that is Igor Lavroff, celebrated his seventeenth birthday. Inga was sent for a whole month along with all the freshmen of the Academy to some incredible wilderness for another training, so I couldn't see her. I ended up celebrating my 17th birthday at home with my mom. Anyway, I was going to move her to Earth, so I thought I'd mix business with a little pleasure. She was a little shocked to find herself the sole owner of the Lavroff Weapons Company, but that's just a little bit. She's already getting used to her son's quirks.

"What am I going to do in the capital, son?" - Mother asked me after she had feasted her eyes upon me and asked me all the usual questions after a long time apart, "This is where I teach the kids, and I like my job. We have a friendly team, an habitual comfortable environment. And what's gonna happen there?"

"And there, Mother, will be the last place the quargs will go if we can't stop them. The capital of the Federation will be defended to the fullest extent possible."

"You're saying terrible things."

"Unfortunately, I am personally familiar with these terrible things. They don't release all the information online to avoid causing panic in the colonies. Right now, the quargs can break anywhere. And as for what you do in the capital, there are also children and elementary schools. You yourself once asked me to move to the Earth."

"I was just trying to talk you out of the idea of becoming a professional military officer," my mother said quietly, "and I was ready to go anywhere for it. I was afraid of losing you."

"And now I'm afraid of losing you. I can't work in peace knowing that you're in danger."

Mother smiled sadly.

"When are we going?"

***

I have carefully read a document that was the product of a collaboration between Leo Rabinovich, Jeff and Professor Stein. The title of the document began with the words 'Cost plan'. That'd be okay, a beautiful document, Rabinovich turned out to be a master at these things, but the amount in the line 'Total' has put my hair on end in all places. 820,000,000 rubles. I could only imagine this sum in the abstract.

The worst part was that even with the most biased approach, I found a way to cut costs by only ten percent, and only by postponing some of the bills when they had a chance to be compensated by the expected revenue from the company's activities.

There's no money, but you hold on! Some of the ancient politicians on Earth said this immortal phrase. My memory has not retained his last name, apparently for the utter uselessness of this individual.

"Gentlemen," I looked up to my comrades, "this is a wonderful plan. But only 30,000,000 rubles are available. We won't even be able to pay advances to the equipment suppliers, I say nothing about everything else."

"You can try leasing equipment," Rabinovich suggested. "This would increase the total by about 10 per cent, but would cut investment by half at the start. But a lot depends on the business reputation of the firm and its owners. How's that working out for you, Igor?"

"I'm afraid that won't do. Although, probably the President's signed license recommendation could help?"

"It's hard to say. You have to try. Although the document certainly inspires respect. But it'll still need a business plan with a forecast of the company's financial flows, a production schedule, justification of the sources of lease payments, and a bunch of mandatory sections up to the background and experience of company executives."

"Even if we can pull this off, we still need to get somewhere almost 400 million more," I voiced my doubts.

"Well, either you have to attract an outside investor, and he, if he gives us the money, is bound to want to be a part owner of the company, or you have to go to the bank for a loan which is about as complex as leasing."

"No, let's try to do without co-owners. This can lead to management problems. All I need is a conflict between shareholders. Prepare the documents, Leo. Tomorrow we'll try our luck at the Federal War Bank. The defense industry enterprises receive credits from this bank, so our subject matter should be close enough, and they have their own leasing company."

***

"Good afternoon, gentlemen. My name is Ilya. I'm the manager of our bank's new clients. How can I help you?" greeted us from the screen of my tablet a short and very thin young man, apparently a small clerk, the main task of whom was to meet first-time clients. It was some kind of filter that was needed to keep nonentities from bothering serious people.

"Good afternoon," answered for us Rabinovich and presented us all. "We represent the Lavroff Weapons Company: development and manufacture of weapons and military equipment.

"I've never heard of your company before. How long have you been in this market?"

"Our company has just received a state license for this activity."

"And what services do you need from our bank?"

"Equipment leasing and working capital replenishment credit. Also your bank account, of course."

"Well, please send me your package of documents."

For ten minutes, the clerk looked at the files he had been given. We waited patiently.

"What can I say, gentlemen," has he finally said, "your company is new, has not yet started and has no experience of successful work in the chosen field. That is a negative, and a very significant one. Your own funds account for only four percent of the loan and lease amounts requested. That's not good either. The sources of repayment of credit and lease payments cannot be considered reliable. If you'd already had contracts with the Ministry of Defense already, it would have been different, after all, you may not win the contest. Those are the downsides. Now, the upsides. You have a very serious license, which means the government thinks your company is well-off and capable of conducting your chosen activities. Besides, you have positive results of combat tests of some of your models, these documents are not standard actually, but this is something. And one last plus: your company has a distinguished scientist and a team of qualified engineers and researchers. All together, the picture is quite contradictory. I'm afraid we won't be able to provide you with the amounts you've asked for."

"Are there any additional factors that could affect the bank's decision?" - I entered into the negotiations.

"Of course. For example, the presence of strong guarantors or a quality collateral whose value exceeds the amount of credit requested."

"Will copyright be a good collateral?"

"This depends on the case and, above all, the amount of royalties in recent months. What do you have to offer?"

"The patent on the treatment of asteroid fever. I've sent you the file."

The manager examined the document for a while and then gave a thoughtful speech:

"Not a bad asset. Of course, it requires a professional appraisal, but I think it's worth around 200 million. That's if it's as a whole. Your share in it is twenty percent... Well, you can get 30 million with this collateral. But as you can see, it doesn't change the situation. Is there anything else?"

"The shares of our company. Given the license, do they have any value as collateral?"

"Unfortunately, it's an illiquid asset. Your shares are not listed on the exchange, so I don't think the bank will be interested in them."

"Tell us, Ilya," Rabinovich has decided to lay down our last trump card, "Have you carefully read the documents relating to our license?"

"Well, I looked at them. They all fit the bill."

"Please note who has signed the license recommendation."

The manager found the document and went into the reading. This time, he looked up to us almost immediately.

"It's very unusual, gentlemen," he spoke with doubt in his voice, "from the point of view of the regulations approved by the bank's board of directors, the identity of the signatory is not a significant factor. But your case is clearly out of line. I'm going to have to submit your application to the director of our branch. He will contact you shortly."

The director of the capital branch of the Federal Military Bank was also unable to make a decision on his own. He contacted us and said that he had given our documents to the board of directors for consideration. They held us for three days, after which we received a categorical rejection from the bank. Not only were we not given the requested amount, we were denied service at all. The head of the branch who told us the news sounded confused and surprised. Either he was a great actor, or he didn't truly understand what had happened. And a new anxious bell rang in my head, and an evil little worm pounded his hammers with a double force.

***

Five other big banks have failed us, too. Two of them categorically refused to deal with us. The others were ready to open accounts for us, and one of them even promised to consider a loan application for 10 million, and the manager assured us that we had every chance of getting approval from the bank management. But it certainly couldn't solve our problem.

Everything became clear on the third day. I was contacted by a confused and clearly upset Rabinovich.

"Igor, I have some bad news for you," he stated directly, "I was approached by people from Global Weapon Industries. They made it clear to me that they wanted to negotiate with the owners of the Lavroff Weapons Company about selling the firm. I'm very interested in working with you, but I want to warn you right now, if you decide not to sell, I will be forced to terminate our business relationship. My business is going to be ruined by such ill-wishers. These are very serious people, and I wouldn't want them to be my opponents."

"Thank you for your candor, Leo," I responded thoughtfully, trying to shape my behavior in new circumstances, "I will not refuse to negotiate. Let's see what these gentlemen have to offer me. Are you still ready to participate at this stage?"

"Until a decision is made to refuse, yes."

"Then arrange a meeting for us, please."

Representatives of one of the world's largest arms manufacturers refused to come to our office. They chose not to invite us to their office either. We met in a neutral area, in the negotiating room of one of the most expensive business centers in the capital.

"So, gentlemen," I took the initiative after our mutual introduction, "You have a proposition for me. I'm listening to you very carefully."

"Igor Yakovlevich," started quietly the Hispanic Enrique Cruz, the first negotiator of the arms corporation, "we are pleased to meet you. Such a young officer, and already a knight of the Gold Star and the Iron Cross. You're a great military man, and obviously that's where you come in."

"Thank you, Mister Cruz," I nodded my head, "but that's clearly not the reason of our meeting."

"Take your time, Mister Lavroff, I was just beginning my thought. So, you're an exemplary officer with incredible combat experience for your age and rank. A brilliant military career awaits you, as you are now a student at the General Staff Academy, and graduation opens many doors to any officer. My colleague Martinez and I would like to understand why do you suddenly need to change your lifestyle abruptly and start a business that you don't know too much about?"

"Gentlemen," I answered with an accentuated surprise in my voice, "but it is more than logical. I was on two combat missions, and in both cases, I was able to achieve high combat effectiveness by improving standard weapons in the service of the Federation Army. Is this not a cause for optimism when we set up our arms business?"

"For optimism? Not at all. You don't seem to know what you're getting yourself into and what you have big ideas about. The development of weapons and military equipment requires enormous resources, both material and human. In addition, this field of activity had long been divided among the major players. We, Global Weapon Industries, have about 40 percent of the arms market. There are three other large corporations, but their shares are lower. And that's it, Mr. Lavroff. There's nobody else around. Of course, small companies do their own developments, but they're not working directly with the Ministry of Defense, they are contractors of a large firm and perform some of their orders. And I can tell you honestly, most of these are either subsidiaries or dependent companies of the same major players in the arms market. But you, bypassing the usual procedures with the full licence to develop and manufacture weapons, have fallen out of this long-established pattern. Nobody needs a new market contestant with direct access to the Ministry of Defense competitions.

"Thanks for the informative tour of the arms business, Mr Cruz," I said with a smile, "So what does the GWI management want from me?"

"We'd like to buy your company. Along with the license, of course, because it's what's most valuable. Our management is ready to offer you 100,000,000 rubles. It's a very good price, Mr. Lavroff. Think of it. In addition, we are prepared to purchase separately all your work already done on the modernization of standard weapons and buy from now on all the promising improvements and new samples that you can create."

Cruz stopped talking, and all three, including Rabinovich, looked at me waiting for an answer. Judging by the look on my consultant's face, he found the GWI's offer more than generous.

"This is a good offer, gentlemen. And if I were an ordinary businessman, I would take it without hesitation."

"What's stopping you, Mr Lavroff?"

"Only one thing. I didn't start this business for profit. I already have enough money to live comfortably. But, alas, not for long. It will be hard for you to understand, gentlemen, I can already see, but still, try, at least to get my motives right to the people you're here for. I just got back from the battle, and I know the reality on the fronts, as I've been moving in the highest military circles, I've been among real high-ranking military commanders. With the available weapons and resources, we will not be able to defeat the quargs, we will lose the war. It's a matter of several years. Who would want the money you promise me for my company? Who would spend it and where?"

"It seems to me, Mr Lavroff, that you are painting the devil blacker than he really is," said Martinez, but it seemed like I was making him uncomfortable, "That's defeatism over the situation…"

"Do I look defeatist to you?" I mildly interrupted the GWI negotiator, "I'm sure you've studied my biography."

"My colleague was wrong to say," Enrique Cruz rushed to smooth things over, "What he really meant was that he himself was more optimistic about the issue. Please continue with your thought."

"Well, gentlemen. I created the Lavroff Weapons Company because I feel I have the power to change the situation. I've picked an excellent team of like-minded people with the necessary expertise. I already have a few promising ideas, which, by my own experience, I believe are the most important for rapid deployment in the Federation Armed Forces. That's what I want to present to the New Equipment and Weapons Commission of the Ministry of Defense. Again. I don't want any profit. Everything I'll earn I plan to put into research and development, and in order for them to be implemented as quickly as possible, I need a direct communication with the Ministry of Defense. I'm gonna do exactly what I think is most relevant to the army right now, and I don't want anyone interfering in this process and dictating to me what is more promising and less so in terms of commercial benefits."

Martinez's face was full of deep-seated disappointment and frustration. He clearly didn't like the negotiations. And Enrique Cruz was thinking about something intensely. Finally, he sighed and looked at me.

"I respect your position, Igor," his voice seemed to express regret, but maybe I just imagined it, "But the reality is, you can't run this business on your own. You've already been turned down for loans and leases? You're a smart man, and I think you've figured out by now that it's not an accident. Trust me, it's only gonna get worse. With all due respect, all sincere respect to your accomplishments, the arms market is not your level. I'm sorry we're on opposite sides of the table, but that's how life turned out, and there's nothing we can do about it. I do recommend that you reconsider our offer. I could double it, but I know it's not about the money. Give up this business and join your team in the GWI. I think I can persuade the management to create a separate unit from your team. You will have virtually unlimited resources and the opportunity to work safely in a large corporation."

"Thank you, Enrique," I thought I'd call him by his first name, "I understand that you're just doing your job, and your employer has given you the task of buying my company. But I can't help you. I need autonomy in decision-making. Complete autonomy, which is absolutely impossible in a vertically integrated corporation like the GWI. So I have to decline. "

"Is that your final decision, Mr Lavroff?" In Martinez's voice, there was an irritation he could barely contain.

"It's final, Mr Martinez."

"Well, I'm afraid you'll soon have to regret that, Second Lieutenant," hissed the negotiator, "'Cause when the Commission of the Ministry of Defense comes to you in three months and sees that there's no real activity going on, it's gonna revoke the license, and all your good intentions will be lost. And without money, you'll have no activity. You may visit all the banks in the Federation, no one will work with you. At most, they'll promise something small and delay for months to make a decision. And if you try to find an outside investor, you know who's going to be behind his back."

"Unfortunately, my colleague is right, Mr Lavroff," - Cruz said mildly, "You have my contact. I'll wait for the call. Our offer still stands. Well, as long as you have a license, of course. Only every day of your delay will reduce the amount offered by us by 2 million rubles. It's been a pleasure meeting you. Now, if you gentlemen will excuse us, we have business to attend to."

***

Not all partners are equally useful. I lost Rabinovich, and I had plans for him.

"I'm sorry, Igor, but if I were you, I'd accept the offer. It's been a pleasure working with you, but I'm afraid you'll have to find another consultant," Rabinovich told me right after the GWI negotiators left.

I didn't feel sorry. It's best to part with an unreliable partner early in a relationship, than to get stabbed in the back later in a more serious situation. Right now, I didn't have time to think of Rabinovich. I had enough problems without him.

I went back to the office, locked myself there, picked up my tablet and started analyzing the situation. Initially, I was going to push into developing new Electronic Warfare stations. Using the knowledge of my civilization, I could quite significantly improve not only the circuits used in the production of electronic warfare equipment, but also the discrete components with which they were assembled. That's what I needed the expensive equipment for. Now I could forget about it, but I can't say that my plans were completely thwarted because of that. After all, there was much that could be done with the Federation's technology, using the software algorithms I knew. Well, we'll improve communications and electronic counteraction systems using what we have.

I looked into the catalogs of the manufacturers and started to figure out exactly what we might need and what amount of money it would cost us. In three months, I have to report to the Commission of the Ministry of Defense and it would be best if I presented a ready-to-act sample. About 40 minutes later, I realized I was stuck and called Jeff in. After spending another hour with him, I realized that it was bad and invited Professor Stein. As a result, our torment resulted in a full meeting of the entire team.

"All right, gentlemen," I've summed it up, "We have found ourselves severely constrained by newly discovered circumstances. It is not possible to purchase expensive research and production equipment at this time, but we have another way. We'll stop the prospective research on new processors for EW stations for now. We're not giving up on them definitively, but since from now on we can only count on ourselves for money, the projects that can prove to the Ministry of Defense our viability and get us a government order become our priority. With money from the realization of the state order we can continue our research."

I looked at my people. They listened to me attentively, but on the faces of the guys whose research issue I put on the back-burner, there was a sour expression.

"Nodir," I told one of them, "don't worry. The processors that you and Jasur have been working over, we will bring them to a successful conclusion, that's for sure. But right now I need you to work on the dynamic interface circuit of EW stations."

"It's all clear to us, Igor Yakovlevich. It's just upsetting when we already saw a breakthrough, or rather, just its shadow on the horizon..."

"You'll have time to break through, don't worry, and for now we continue our business. In three months, I want to present to the Commission of the Ministry of Defense a commando platoon equipped with our new camouflage equipment. Three dropships, three light combat robots Goanna-M2 and a set of combat space suits I'll try to borrow from the Planetary Commando Academy along with a platoon of cadets, and we'll have to buy the rest with the company's money. Chief Engineer Jeff and I have worked out a scheme of how to assemble the equipment. So far, these are just sketches that have yet to be finalized, and it's up to you to do it. In a couple of days, I'm gonna finish writing a program that will make all this hardware work in the way we want it. Again, it is certain that adjustments will have to be made to it, as it is not yet clear what ambushes will be encountered along the way. Chief Engineer and Professor Stein will assign current tasks to all staff. In two days, I want a complete list of equipment and components we're gonna need. Keep in mind that you only need to ask for the essentials, because our resources are not latex and stretch badly."

And yet there was not enough money. By cutting as much as we could, and sometimes more that we could, we managed to put the cost within 50 million. I was well aware that there should be some margin for contingencies, so it took 60 million to do the right thing, of which I've only had 30 so far.

The money issue was solved in a way that was unexpected. Ivan Gerkhardovich came to my office later this evening. The professor seemed to be contemplative, but I could see that he didn't just come here to discuss the current affairs.

"Igor, I've been thinking about the amount of money we need," he went straight to the point, "GWI has forced the banks to refuse our company loans, that's understandable. But you and I can act not on behalf of the Lavroff Weapons Company, but simply as ordinary citizens. Obviously, in the banks where we've been before, they won't talk to us, But there's a small bank on Titan, the Russian Credit Union of Titan. I've had an account there for a long time. This bank serves the Colonial Technological Institute, so I became their client for convenience."

I was looking at the professor and I couldn't believe it. Careful and conservative Ivan Gerkhardovich impressed me with his «you and I» when he talked about credit.

"Professor, did I hear that? Do you want to join me as a loan debtor?"

"Well, probably not a loan debtor after all. I'm not ready for that yet. But I'm ready to be a pawnor and a guarantor. Don't forget, I also own 20% of our asteroid fever patent and I, though I am an old greedy person and scientific go-getter, I know in my heart who's really in charge of this patent. But it's not just that, Igor. I don't want you to fail. I remember well what you said to convince me to move into your firm. In ten years, I'd like to go home to Titan and teach the students of the Colonial Technological Institute again. But to do that, I have to have a place to come back. So you can count on my share as collateral, which is an additional 30 million, I understand."

***

Before that, we communicated with the banks exclusively through the network, but at the Russian Credit Union of Titan, the professor and I decided to appear in person. The flight to Titan did not take long, and the next day Ivan Gerkhardovich and I sat in the office of the manager. The professor turned out to be a long-standing and respected client of the bank. Ivan Gerkhardovich received regular royalties, which he did not spend in a hurry, so the bank was very pleased with this client.

After listening to us and looking at the documents, the manager smiled.

"Gentlemen, I hope you understand that the interest rate on consumer credit will be higher than if you approached me as company representatives?"

"Of course, Mr Kamsky, we are aware of this" - I answered his allusion that he was aware of the situation around the Lavroff Weapons Company, "but at the moment, the idea of turning to you on behalf of the firm does not seem to us to be a good one."

"I think you're right, and it's very nice that you came to us. You were doubly right to come to the bank in person. Right now, no one can hear us, so I'm willing to be frank. Our board of directors is very interested in you, Mr Lavroff. We see how you achieve your goals and see the results, especially the financial ones, because that is the nature of our activities, that your efforts can bring.

For known reasons, we wouldn't be able to issue a loan to the Lavroff Weapons Company, but we will reply favourably to you personally, as a citizen of the Federation, a dweller of Titan, and a knight of the Gold Star and the Iron Cross.

We are more than satisfied with your offer of bail. We can always implement such a patent if your venture fails. But, in granting such a loan, although we are not formally in conflict with forces known to you, we do bear certain risks associated with their possible reaction to helping you. So we'd like you to do us a favor."

"I'm listening to you very carefully, Ivan Denisovich."

"If, as a result of our cooperation, the Lavroff Weapons Company gets access to state orders and will take its rightful place in the arms market, we'd like it to switch to our bank. All I need from you is a simple promise."

"And what do you think, Ivan Denisovich, to which bank would I take my company after only one of the people I approached came into my position and agreed to help? I don't even have to promise you anything. I was going to do that."

"Well, gentlemen. Then we can move on to formalities."

***

Lieutenant General Shiller listened to me with a gloomy look on his face. I didn't hide anything from him. This man has helped me more than once, and I didn't expect him to stab me in the back.

"Second Lieutenant", he said when I shut up, "you're taking a big risk. These people aren't going to make jokes. Are you sure you've considered everything?"

"Am I risking more than on Leiten-5, General, Sir?"

"Don't pretend to be stupid, Lavroff. These are different risks. No one will kill you, at least with their own hands. But you started a case that you have no right to fail. I hope you understand that as well as I do. Except the GWI leadership doesn't care about your motives. I don't know what they think, but I believe that greed really caught their eye. And I know what their next move will be. If you present the Commission something worth mentioning, their lobbyists will insist on combat tests before the state contract, and you and your men and your new equipment will be sent to a place from which you won't return. Are you ready for this?"

"I suspected something like this. I guess I'll just have to go through that."

"Are you that sure of yourself?"

"I am confident in myself, in my men, and in the cadets of the Planetary Commando Academy I'd like to ask of you for the duration of the state acceptance of my new equipment. What we submit to the test site will be a breakthrough technology enough to interest the Commission, but we will not show them everything. I'm gonna put something up my sleeve to get that trump card during the battle trials, no matter how difficult the conditions. We'll get thru this."

"I wouldn't believe anyone else, but I know you as an officer who won't talk in vain. I'll try to help you, Second Lieutenant. But that decision will have to be agreed with the board of trustees. At least with its head. I think General Vasnetsov will support me."

Chapter 3

I only had a month before the General Staff Academy. All this time, ever since the Gold Star award, I've been on vacation, as I had already finished the Planetary Commando Academy early, and the order was for me to come to the General Staff Academy only on June 20th. Well, I was supposed to be on leave, after the award.

For most of this month, I've been between the capital and Ganymede, where Jeff and four of our engineering students were poking around in the Academy repair depot. The general didn't let me down, and Vasnetsov turned out to be an understanding person.

Anyway, I've been given the least damaged equipment. A couple of times, Shiller personally came down to the hangar and silently watched us suffer without interfering in the process, and the next day, without saying a word, he sent us a team of three Academy technicians to help us. There was a lot of work to be done because we were going to equip with our new EW stations not only dropships and Goannas but also the armored spacesuites of paratroopers. We're gonna smash it!!! All elements of a commando platoon must meet the new requirements of invisibility.

By the end of the month, I was able to catch my breath, when I realized that the guys under the sensitive guidance of Lieutenant Jeff and Professor Stein could follow thru without my direct involvement, and I flew to the capital on June 19th. The General Staff Academy was waiting for me.

***

The grey-haired Colonel, to whom I reported my arrival, was surprised seeing my Second Lieutenant's shoulder straps, but after discerning the qualifying tab, the Gold Star and the Iron Cross, refrained from comment and silently accepted my documents. After checking the lists on his tablet, he sent me the key code to my new room, and instructions on where and when to attend the presentation ceremony to the Chief of the Academy. The formalities ended, which I was delighted to hear.

At the General Staff Academy, the students were treated very differently from the cadets at the Planetary Commando Academy. Well, of course, we were all officers with considerable combat experience, who distinguished themselves in battles and managed to command sufficiently serious units. My room resembled a room in a nice hotel. As it turned out, the service here was almost the same. We fed in the dining-hall, which was not inferior to some restaurants in terms of interior decoration and the finesse of the waiters. The future elite of the Federation Armed Forces was valued here.

And, of course, there was no barrack status with the layoffs and all the nice stuff around here. Trainees were required to attend classes and examinations on time, the rest of their life was not regulated, except in emergency situations, of course.

At the ceremony, I was openly looked askance at. I've never seen an officer below the rank of captain here, but met more than a dozen lieutenant colonels among the audience, then lost count and gave it up. I was not impressed by the speech of the General of the Army O'Sullivan, Academy Chief. It was felt that the elderly Irishman was no longer a military man, but rather an administrator. What awaits us within these walls, I knew it already, so I listened him lending half an ear.

After the ceremony, everyone went to our dining room for the inaugural dinner. I haven't met anyone here yet, so I humbly took a seat at one of the back tables and began to await developments. Events have not slowed down.

Two majors and a captain, saying something not quite clear, which should have meant 'You don't mind, Second Lieutenant?' sat comfortably at my table. Judging by their behavior, they've known each other for a long time. I just had to figure out what they wanted with me, 'cause there was plenty of tables left.

"Good morning, officers," I was the first to greet them as a junior officer, but I certainly did not stand up and salute them because the atmosphere was different.

"Good morning, Second Lieutenant," responded one of two majors who stood out with an expressive double chin.

Maybe I was wrong, but I thought he was on some kind of weak drug. There wasn't any alcohol scent from the Major, but there was a lot of drugs to buy in the capital...

"Come on, Second Lieutenant, don't sweat it. It's a dinner party, an informal setting..." The second major, who looked visibly more fit and athletic than his comrade, entered the conversation.

"Gentlemen," - I have not accepted the officers' presumptuous tone, "do you have business with me? If you just like this table so much, I can get another seat, I don't mind."

"Tell me, Second Lieutenant," - joined the conversation a short captain who looked a few years younger than the majors, "at this age and at that rank, how can you become a student of the General Staff Academy? My comrades and I had an argument about whose protégé you were, and we never agreed. Okay, if you're 18 years old, even though you look younger. But you've already done the fighting, and judging by the tab, it's a hell of a fight. Gold Star for what?"

"Leiten-5," I answered briefly, not wishing to develop the conversation, but without provoking conflict.

"Well, it wasn't that hard. Our strategists expected far greater losses. Come on, and what about the Iron Cross? It's a soldier's reward, even though it's high."

"Kapteen. A rescue mission in no man's land."

"You're laconic, Second Lieutenant," the fat Major intervened again, "You don't want to talk to us?"

"And what do you think, officers, Sirs? I don't know you, you sit down at my table without even asking if I want you here, start talking to me like I'm an old friend who's already drunk with you more than a bucket, and even without introducing yourselves, ask frankly provocative questions. Would you like all this?"

"Well, Second Lieutenant, you're being sassy. You're a few ranks and a dozen years younger than us. Who should be the first to introduce himself?"

"Those who are fishing for acquaintance, I suppose. The situation, as you rightly pointed out, is unofficial."

"Just answer the question who pushed you in here, and we'll go. We don't need anything else from you, and we're not interested in you," pronounced the Captain in a much tougher voice, and from his movements and his intonations, it was finally clear to me that he, too, had some chemical product in his blood.

"Officers, Sirs, don't you find your words out of bounds?" I showed how good I am at letting steel in my voice.

"Just answer the question," it was the Major with the binary chin.

"Have fun staying, gentlemen. I'm not interested in this place anymore," I got up and headed for the exit. After all, I could have dinner in my room and I was busy today.

The fat Major twitched towards me, but the Captain silently held his hand and quietly said: "Second Lieutenant, quarrelling with us is bad for your career. You better remember it. Soon you will feel the full justice of those words on yourself."

I didn't react. Why? Well, the idiots in all the excitement are enjoying some dope. They'll sleep it off and it'll all go away. However, it didn't.

***

I always knew fate was a very ironic lady, and her irony sometimes takes on the most unexpected forms. When I saw our entire group at the first lesson of troops strategic management, I wasn't even surprised by three insolently smirking faces, which I had the good fortune to see at my table last night. I really do possess pronounced properties of getting into trouble. And in my previous life I was the same...

"Officers, Sirs," young-looking Colonel General Swirsky, our strategist instructor, took a close look around the group, "today you have an introductory class. We'll look into the last major battle in which our army and fleet stopped the enemy's advance, but unfortunately suffered great losses and were forced to abandon the star system Gliese-338. This is the battle I'm going to use to introduce you to our training equipment, which simulates the strategic management of ground forces and fleets. At the end of the session, each of you will complete a task that will demonstrate to you the complexity and many-sidedness of the management of large military formations. This task will not be a test, nor will it be evaluated, it will only help you to get acquainted with the training complex. But we'll examine the results of your efforts. You are to serve as one of the commanders in the very battle of Gliese, and then we'll compare your results to what happened in real combat, but we'll talk about that later."

And the General told us what really happened in the star systems of Gliese and Grumbridge, with all the details that didn't leak into the network news or even into the special reports from the fronts intended only for officers. Here at the General Staff Academy, our access to information was infinitely higher than most officers had outside its walls.

And it was very bad there. The systems were completely unprepared to repel the enemy's massive strike.

Around the dim red star, component A of the binary star Gliese-338, there were almost one and a half dozen different planets, three of which were partially terraformed 30 years ago. On the basis of these, the

Federation Armed Forces have constructed the main points of defence of the system. The orbital fortresses, built 15 years ago and upgraded a couple of times since, represented a fairly serious force, not to fear the capture of planets by surprise attack. Over each of the major planets, there were four of them. A fleet of five battleships, a dozen cruisers, two aircraft carriers, and half a hundred destroyers and corvettes appeared strong enough to give the defenses the necessary flexibility.

Quargs regularly tried to probe the approaches to Gliese, as well as to its neighbor, the star system of Grumbridge, but no serious attacks were ever made. However, the Federation Seventh Fleet had deployed a dense network of mobile space control systems in the vicinity of both stars, and even patrolled the remote outlying areas using several dozen of the most modern corvettes, equipped with still very expensive and not very reliable hyperfield scanners, theoretically capable of detecting yet-to-come-out-of-hyperjump enemy ships.

When the counter-attack on Leiten-5 was being prepared in the 'crisis-mode' style, the Fifth Strike Fleet was reinforced with many additional forces, but these forces had to come from somewhere. As a result, Gliese and Grumbridge's defense systems lost most of the very modern ships that provided reconnaissance for the outlying areas.

Later analysis suggested that it was highly probable that the quargs had used in this offensive their latest developments in the concealment of ships, which were 10-15% more effective than the Federation Fleet had encountered so far. The combination of these two factors led the Seventh Fleet to oversleep the appearance of a squadron of quargs in the Gliese system.

The surprise of the strike allowed the quargs to capture the main Federation Fleet forces at medium alert, and most importantly, they were scattered throughout the system. This led to the need for groups of ships to enter the battle in parts, which allowed the quargs to create points of local balance in forces that sometimes reached the ratio of one to ten. The quarg fleet, which outnumbered the Federation forces in heavy ships and aircraft carriers at least twice, gained a decisive advantage, and by the time the battle had moved into the high orbits of the planets, only one third of the original Seventh Fleet was able to rise under the cover of orbital fortresses.

Grumbridge's situation was similar, but there were markedly fewer quargs.

Subsequently, military analysts concluded that the strike in this direction was distracting and debilitating. It's goal was to stop people from moving reinforcements to the attacked planets in the Gliese system, but even in this weakened form, the attack on Grumbridge caused serious losses and destruction.

Meanwhile, the Seventh Fleet, pressed against planets and orbital fortresses, continued to resist, although the outcome of the battle was already determined.

There were significant ground forces on the planets, but they couldn't help their dying comrades in space. The limits of their firepower are low orbits. The anti-orbital missile launchers were waiting for their turn, when the quarg landing forces descend into the corridors cut thru the defenders.

This hour had come fast enough, despite the fact that the Seventh Fleet had died all to the last ship, trying to prevent the enemy from clearing its way down to the planets. After the destruction of the mobile space forces, the orbital fortresses evolved from defensive strongholds into powerful, low-mobility ships, which were still fighting off enemy attacks but were already unable to prevent the landing, and, above all, to hinder the enemy fleet from launching low-altitude attacks on ground troops. Under these conditions, the quargs quickly destroyed anti-orbital devices placed on the surface, they didn't take into account the losses that ended up not being so great.

Further, the planetary forces were unable to counteract the enemy landing forces. The quargs simply bypassed their nests of resistance, and then destroyed them from orbit. That's what happens when the space over planet is controlled by one of the belligerents.

General Swirsky ceased speaking, and there was gloomy silence in the audience. All the officers here knew what a real fight was, and imagined themselves in the place of dying comrades, knowing that their deaths can no longer make a difference in a hopeless situation.

"After the battle, the course of the combat was thoroughly analyzed, both by analysts and by specialized computer programs," - Swirsky again spoke, "The failure of intelligence operations is obvious and not in doubt, as a result, the appearance of the enemy fleet from the hyperspace within the Gliese system came as a complete surprise to the defence forces. They were supposed to have been discovered on a previous emergence in the vicinity of the system or shortly before the last exit. But it turned out the way it did. But what the Fleet and the planetary defense forces did next is highly judged by the analysts.

The mobile space forces were commanded by Admiral Berkovich, and after his death by Vice Admiral Stravinsky. The combat effectiveness of their defense management is estimated at 82% of the best result, received by computer analysis of various battle scenarios. Ground troops had noticeably less room for maneuver and decision-making, because they were put in a position of near hopelessness from the beginning. Planetary defense of the fourth, fifth and seventh planets of the system was commanded by Lieutenant Generals Sanders, Lewinsky and Grigoriev, respectively. Their operational effectiveness ranges from 70 to 75% of the optimum. In any case, under all scenarios analysed, even with optimal fleet and ground command, we would lose the Gliese-338 system."

What happened next, I knew that. The Fifth Strike Fleet, battered in the battle of Leiten-5 and hastily diverted to the attacked systems, first headed for Groombridge. The quargs did not take the fight and rushed out of the system, jumping towards Gliese. And when Admiral Nelson led his ships there, it was clear that there was no one left to help, the system was completely overrun by the enemy and was hastily preparing for defense. After calculating the force ratio, Nelson asked the command for further action and was ordered to return to Groombridge.

"So, officers, Sirs, I've briefed you on the course of the battle," continued Swirsky, "Now for the practical part of our class we'll go to the Strategic Scenario Simulator."

The room next door to our auditorium turned out to be a vast hall, In the centre of which a large projection screen was placed in front of the rows of seats, a three-dimensional image of the Academy logo was running on the screen, and around the perimeter there were some grey-steel cubes, as it turned out, they were the highlights of this place.

General Swirsky pressed something on the screen of his tablet and the doors opened in the cubes.

"Officers, Sirs, take your seats in the simulators. You'll get all the explanations inside."

The simulator turned out to be a very interesting device. From the inside, it resembled something between a ship's command post and a cabin of the planetary forces' command and staff machine. From Swirsky's explanation, we have learned that the table that occupied half of the free space is, in fact, a huge tablet of command, on which a three-dimensional tactical projection is drawn, as appropriate, liaison windows with units and subunits, various diagrams and graphs showing the current status and movement of troops, loss figures and other relevant information.

As in real life, commands could be given by voice or by moving pictograms on the tactical projection. The simulator independently generated the reports of the subordinate commanders and in every way simulated the actual combat management, and the three-dimensional screen, which occupied the entire wall above the tablet table, showed the course of the simulated battle, where any detail could be highlighted if desired. Well, it wasn't that hard to understand how it worked.

When all the participants confirmed their readiness for the task of study, we heard again the voice of General Swirsky:

"Now, officers, you will all have the same task, which will take you two to three hours real time. I'm talking about real time, because the simulated battle lasted three days, but we don't have the opportunity to spend three days in simulators. Therefore, the fragments of battle between making your key decisions and giving the necessary orders you can view in accelerated mode.

All actions of our troops and enemy the simulator models in the most detailed way, based on the extensive statistics we have accumulated and analysed on combat engagements with quargs. We know the tactics of the enemy, as well as the fact that the quargs rarely retreat from their tactical patterns, which certainly makes it easier for us to model a battle.

So, in a few minutes, each of you will be playing Lieutenant General Sanders, leading the planetary forces on Gliese-4. You will find yourself in the situation when the quarg fleet entered the system. In addition to the planetary forces, all four orbital fortresses will be under your command and that part of the Seventh Fleet that was in real battle orbiting Gliese-4 at the time of the approach to the planet of the quarg space forces. And so does the civil administration of the planet, in case you need anything from it. Otherwise, beyond your influence, the battle will proceed as it did in reality. Your job is to do maximum damage to the enemy. I hope you can come closer to the results achieved by Lieutenant General Sanders, who perished heroically in this battle.

Prepare yourselves, gentlemen, in 30 seconds the combat simulation mode will be activated."

The screen in front of my eyes was softly illuminated and displayed a tactical projection. In the upper right corner, columns of information about the forces of the quargs invading the system were already alarmingly running.

I took a look at the map of the coming hostilities and put on the screen a list of the troops at my disposal. Under my command was an infantry corps, reinforced by two divisions of heavy robots Bison-K4. In addition, I had 40 mobile anti-orbital missile launchers and nearly 300 atmospheric pursuit planes and attack planes. That was directly on the planet. And besides, four orbital fortresses, to which a badly damaged battleship, a near-dead aircraft carrier, a comparatively well-preserved cruiser, and a dozen smaller ships would eventually join.

As I recall from General Swirsky's report, the quargs will press the remnants of the Seventh Fleet down to the planets in about six hours. I was hoping I'd have enough time to carry out the plan conceived.

I looked at the list of my troops and I clearly understood what a formidable force it was. But I did remember that 80% of the planetary forces died in Gliese-4 not in combat with the landed quargs, but under orbital strikes.

At present, I had at my disposal troops that were numerically inferior to all the landing forces that the quargs brought with them into the system, only one and a half times, and if I wanted to achieve an acceptable result, I had to force the enemy to fight them on an equal footing, and better yet, under the conditions I'll be able to impose on the enemy.

In my past life, we'd been at war with toads for so long that we'd had all kinds of combat situations. There was a case like this in our military history, though not similar in every detail. The similarity was that, in the defense of the planet, the ground force was very strong, and in contrast, orbital defense was almost useless.

The decision taken at that time by the planetary forces commander is still considered controversial by our analysts, but then it worked, and the winners, as you know, don't go to jail. And now I've decided to take advantage of my past.

"Orbital fortresses, begin a maneuver to change position," I gave my first order in this virtual battle, and backed it up by indicating the new locations for my most formidable space weapon on the tactical projection. 'I'm gonna get the fuck out of here' - that optimistic thought came into my head, but I sent it to the right place: very far away.

After calling a map of the planet to the screen, I began to give my troops orders to change positions. I finished by ordering the Chief of Civil Administration to begin the evacuation of the population to the square I indicated, and even provided them with a transport battalion. This process took me ten minutes, then I activated the conditional-time acceleration mode.

The barely noticeable movement of the heavy and awkward orbital fortresses has turned into a swift flight, the markings of ground troops and air units started to rush about the screen at a frenzied speed, and the numbers on the clock began to gallop. Two minutes later, I stopped a raging race of time, and I was in an absolutely different strategic situation.

From the point of view of the man entrusted with the defense of the planet, my actions were a monumental folly, if not a crime. In fact, I was surrendering the planet to the enemy without a fight. But it was already clear that the quargs would take over the planet, so why burn my already small space forces in a hopeless attempt to prevent the quargs from landing? I decided to do the opposite.

The standard position of the four orbital fortresses was considered to be at the vertices of the tetrahedron into which the planet's ball was inscribed. But such a scheme is good for the protection of the entire surface and is effective in the presence of serious fleet forces, for which fortresses play the role of centers of resistance. In this case, I had virtually no fleet, and the distant orbital fortresses could not provide tangible support to each other.

A squadron large enough is really able to bind an orbital fortress by battle to such an extent, that it will lose the ability to control low orbits in its area of responsibility, what happened in the real battle of Gliese-4. The powerful and heavily armed fortresses did not have a significant impact on the course of the battle.

I decided to use them all together. I have chosen a relatively small surface area, where there were many ammunition depots, fixed anti-space defence systems and other military infrastructure, I ordered the fortresses to change the current anchorage points and line up a square above this section of the surface. This was where I relocated my entire corps with reinforcements, and assembled the civilian population of the planet into the centre of the protected area, I mean, those citizens who had time to reach there. All the ships that came to the planet have taken up positions inside the square of the orbital fortresses, so they reinforced a pretty tight defense.

My maneuvers were based on a fairly simple idea. If I have a powerful planetary group comparable in strength to the enemy, why would I waste my forces trying to prevent an enemy landing? The only reason for this is to protect the civilian population. This argument is more than serious. But when you look at the real balance of power, it turns out to be untenable. In trying to protect everyone, we inevitably lose everybody, and in my version, there's a chance to save at least a fraction of the people who have time to evacuate. The main reason I acted was to prevent the enemy from shooting my troops from orbit during the battle, instead, to have our own ships above our heads. Under these conditions, it will be very difficult for the quargs to scratch off my foothold.

It was really a bridgehead, because both we and the quargs knew very well that somewhere in the interior of space the Fifth Strike Fleet is now heading toward the systems under attack, speeding up the engines, and a piece of the planet's surface, controlled by Federation troops, will be very useful for this fleet in organizing a counter-offensive.

The battle has begun. Now, my orders were of little consequence. Every soldier knew his maneuver, and the battle was waged without my involvement.

I've rerun the accelerated mode.

The quargs have dropped their landing forces with lightning speed, and, while paying no attention to the people who tried to conceal themselves, they rushed into battle. And they washed in their own blood. A barrage of heavy weapons fire, which met them, mixed their advanced forces with the ground. Orbital fortresses and ships hovering above our heads played a significant role in this process.

The quargs decided then to come from the other side. They took the landed units to regroup, and hit our orbital umbrella with fleet forces. They didn't like the result. It's one thing to bind by battle a single orbital fortress, which several ships badly beaten in the previous combat are trying to cover up, and it is quite different to stand under the well coordinated salvos of four armored giants which are capable of knocking out a battleship with their concentrated fire in ten minutes.

I looked at the chronometer. By this point in the actual battle, the quargs had already torn Sanders' corps apart and killed remaining units from orbit. Of course, the rest of the troops tried to fight for another 48 hours, but it was more like guerrilla action. Resistance on the fifth and seventh planets, where the number of Federation troops was lower than on Gliese-4, was finally suppressed within the first 24 hours, and I was expecting for the quargs to draw their forces from the whole system to my foothold.

And they did. The space forces of the quargs, augmented by ships coming from the fifth and seventh planets, launched an attack at the same time as another ground assault began. Their plan didn't shine bright by its originality, but it was as difficult to resist as a blow of an iron crowbar. Fortresses and ships could no longer support the ground forces. There was so much deadly iron flying towards them, that anti-missile systems and high-velocity guns of direct defense hardly managed to destroy even the most dangerous targets. Some of the shells and rockets still burst on the thick armour of the fortresses, and sometimes also on the ships.

The first to fail was the aircraft carrier badly damaged in the previous battle. Having releaseed into space the few remaining pursuit planes of its wing, it started to dive out of orbit faster and faster, and fall into the planet's gravity well. Multiple damage reports came in from the orbital fortresses, the battleship nearly ceased fire and was forced to hide behind the hull of one of the fortresses.

The cruiser was still fighting, but it seemed to be getting harder to stay in service by the minute.

The quargs were also being hard hit. Their streamers were extinguished on the tactical projection one by one. Still, four orbital fortresses standing next to each other - on space standards - are capable of giving away such a density of fire in a coordinated salvo, that would be hell for any heavy ship.

And on the surface, the quargs were storming our fortified area. Our enemies have gathered their forces from the conquered planets on Gliese-4 and launched a decisive offensive. Their numerical superiority, of course, affected the course of the combat, but without orbital support, they were not the same quargs that easily overran Sanders' corps in real battle.

We held on. The Bisons were very good. Here I had to slow down the time run to almost the normal speed, and personally direct the tactics of the heavy robot divisions, shutting down the impending breakthroughs. We didn't even think about any counterstrikes. My troops should not have protruded from under the orbital umbrella, but we held on to our territory as best we could.

And at some point, the quargs ran out of steam. It cost us almost the entire orbital grouping. Now our bridgehead, which had shrunk almost twice, was covered by the ruins of two fortresses, that held together somehow, a barely surviving battleship and a badly damaged cruiser. There was nothing else left. Three quarters of the Bisons fell in battle, the Infantry Corps was reduced to an incomplete division, 300 atmospheric pursuit planes and attack planes left two dozen ready to fight. But the guarg forces have also come to an end. Apparently, their concept of strategy and tactics did not allow them to throw in the final force. They had to understand that humans wouldn't leave things as they are, and a counterstrike on Gliese-338 was more than possible.

I looked at the chronometer. It's been five days since the attack began. I've accelerated the time, and on the eighth day of our standing at the bridgehead, scanners from the least-affected fortress detected the emergence of Admiral Nelson's Fifth Strike Fleet out of hyper-space.

Tactical projection has extinguished, in its place appeared a large inscription 'Time has expired. The execution of the training task has been stopped'. I looked at my watch. I've been inside the simulator for three and a half hours. That was more than General Swirsky gave us to complete the task.

I opened the door and went out into the hall. All of my group mates were already sitting in the chairs in front of the projection screen, listening attentively, as the General commented on the actions of another officer. I went quietly, took a seat in the back row and tried to get a sense of what was going on.

"So, Major Linden," Swirsky told the double-chined officer standing by the screen. Judging by the tone of his voice, he wasn't too satisfied. "Your combat efficiency is below 45 %. Do you know what your mistake was?"

"Not yet, Colonel General, Sir," Linden replied, indicating a slight shrug of shoulders, that, in my opinion, with such a difference in rank, was completely unacceptable behavior, "In accordance with my task, I sought to inflict maximum damage on the enemy."

To my surprise, the General ignored the Major's gesture, as if he hadn't even noticed it. "You counter-attacked the landed enemy troops in a situation where this could not be done under any circumstances, Major," patiently explained Swirsky, "You were unable to provide air cover for your Bisons, and you hadn't done any preliminary reconnaissance of the enemy forces. As a result, you lost 90% of your heavy robots, and your troops suffered heavy losses having achieved only local success without inflicting adequate losses on the enemy. Is that clear, Major Linden?"

"That's right, Colonel General, Sir," said Linden with a sour look on his face. He didn't seem interested in what Svirsky said. Who is he, after all, if he allows himself such behavior with a superior officer and is not afraid of the consequences?

"Take your place, Major. Let's move on to the next commander," pronounced the General with a slight sarcasm, looking at me, "I see we're already full assembly. You're a little late, Second Lieutenant. It was necessary to use more of the accelerated time regime."

"That's right, Colonel General, Sir," I answered, rising from my seat.

"Don't stretch, Second Lieutenant," the General grinned, "You are at the General Staff Academy. This is not a parade ground."

"That's right, Colonel General, Sir," I answered more calmly, "Let me explain the reason for the delay?"

"There's no need, Second Lieutenant, we'll see it ourselves," said the General and made something with his tablet. On the screen appeared a tactical projection reflecting the initial phase of the battle. The General has set off an accelerated time, and the objects on it started to move. Surprised to track the redeployment of fortresses and troops, the General stopped the reproduction.

"What does it mean, Second Lieutenant? What have you done?"

"I have redeployed my troops to a fortified bridgehead and secured a solid orbital defence umbrella over it. I have also evacuated parts of the planet's population to the central part of the bridgehead."

"That's what I can see without you," General Swirsky's annoyingly pronounced, "Do you realize we're not playing games here, Second Lieutenant? Do you realize what you've done? You have exposed the defences of an entire planet, abandoning its people, which we have sworn to defend with all our might. Do you understand that?"

"That's right, Colonel General, Sir. It was with that understanding that I acted."

"Explain yourself!"

"With the current force ratio, it's impossible to protect the entire planet. That's what all the calculations show. We can stand to the death, as the heroically perished Lieutenant General Sanders brilliantly demonstrated, but we can't protect the planet and its entire population. I had two goals: to save the part of the population that could evacuate to the bridgehead, and stop the quargs from firing on my troops from orbit, and force them to attack under adverse conditions."

"Now I'm going to play it, Second Lieutenant," the General said with an ice-cold voice, "and if what I see doesn't convince me, I will be forced to draw conclusions as to the extent to which you meet the status of a student at the Academy."

The image on the screen started to move. The quargs landed unhindered on the planet's surface and launched an attack. Sometimes the General would turn on accelerated time, but all in all, we spent about five hours watching the virtual battle.

It's been a long time since it was dark behind the windows, some officers looked in our room a couple of times, but when they saw the General's grim face, they quietly disappeared, covering the door behind them.

In that time, Swirsky didn't say a word. When scanners of a dilapidated orbital fortress detected the ships of the Fifth Strike Fleet in the system, playback stopped due to the end of the time allocated for the task. The Colonel General still silently did something on the tablet, and the image came back to life, unfolding before us a chain of events that never happened in our reality.

Colonel General Swirsky looked at the screen, clenching his fists. His cheekbones showed how much he had clenched his teeth, and his eyes were shining in a wrong way.

"We blew our chance, officers, Sirs," finally squeezed out the General, with bitterness in his voice, watching the markings of quarg ships extinguish on tactical projection under the strikes of Admiral Nelson's fleet, and as the landing transports approach the still standing bridgehead, which Lieutenant General Sanders' corps never surrendered to the enemy. Unfortunately, only the virtual corps of the General who died in real combat.

"The class is over, everyone is free." It was as if a rod had been pulled out of Swirsky, which held all his tranquillity and confidence. The General has fallen hard into the chair at his desk, "Second Lieutenant Lavroff, hold on."

"Second Lieutenant," Swirsky pronounced tiredly when the door closed behind the last officer of our group, "I'll be forced to forward the file of your battle to the General Staff Analysis Center. It's too important information to soft-pedal it. You have achieved extraordinary combat effectiveness in the training mission, but the method you used smells like a crime. Gliese-4 is a small and sparsely populated planet, but you gave it to the Quargs without a fight along with 40 million Federation citizens. I understood the Civil Administration had evacuated about a million people to your foothold."

"Colonel General, Sir, is a million people rescued worse than a completely lost population of the entire planet?"

"It's not worse, Second Lieutenant, moreover, in the situation that has arisen in the training mission, the quargs would simply not have had sufficient time to commit genocide, and I'm sure if this were the case, at least half the people on the planet would survive. But it's not that. These are dry numbers, but there's a notion of military honor. You can't leave civilians to be massacred by the enemy. You just can't. Never. Even if the army suffers huge and seemingly unjustifiable losses."

I understood the General. He was from the old school that had been formed before the war with the quargs. He remembered a peaceful life and his notions of the honor of an officer came from there. Twenty years of war haven't changed that.

"Colonel General, Sir, this war does not raise before us the question of the loss of territories or the temporary cessation of expansion," I said firmly, looking Swirsky in the eye, "The question is whether humans will survive as a species, or whether only quargs will remain in the galaxy. We no longer have military and civilians. Those concepts have gone with a peaceful life and with the latest unsuccessful attempts to deal with the enemy. We are all soldiers now, even children and the elderly people, even if not all of us have realized this. There is no more abstract humanism. All that remains is combat effectiveness. And it's the only thing that can ultimately be the ideal for any officer, at least until the war with the quargs ends with our victory. You can see that even in this particular training mission my cynicism and cruelty ended up being the most humane solution of all possibilities."

"Perhaps my views are outdated, Second Lieutenant, and I'm ready to admit it. I see that if all three of the planetary commanders used your tactics, we could defend the system and save the lives of most of the population. I understand your position, and I'm even prepared to accept that this is the only way to wage this war, but my notion of officer's honor do not allow me to accept it, and I'm sure a lot of officers at the General Staff would agree with me."

"I myself agree in many ways with your assessment, Colonel General, but I have a goal - winning the war, and I'm ready to push the rest of it into the back of my mind. In real combat, I would have done what I did in this training mission. When I win, my conscience will show me all the bills I put away. That's when I have an opportunity to evaluate my actions in terms of ethics and honor, but not before. And if anyone asks me what would lead humanity to victory, humanism or the density of fire of my troops, I will not hesitate to choose the density of fire."

"Where did you get your battle experience in senior command positions, Second Lieutenant?" - Swirsky changed the subject.

"Leiten-5, Colonel General, Sir. I commanded the Heavy Commando Brigade."

"Second Lieutenant was a Brigade Commander?"

"I was a cadet of the Planetary Commando Academy back then. There were just no other candidates in that situation."

"Is that where the Gold Star came from?"

"That's right, Colonel General, Sir."

"Now, at least I understand why you were so confident in making decisions in training mission. You are a good officer, Second Lieutenant. A real fighter charged to win. In an accompanying letter to the training mission materials that I'll send to the General Staff, I'll give your acting a positive evaluation, although I don't share much of your point of view. It's a pity that fewer students like you are joining our Academy, and more and more untouchable deadbeats like this Major Linden, who shouldn't be allowed to enter the command of the troops, but is backed by the industrial-military lobby."

"Your permissilon to ask a question, Colonel General, Sir?"

"Go on."

"Is Major Linden really so untouchable? What will happen to the man who confronts him?"

By the look on the General's face, I knew he was regretting ever bringing up the subject of Linden and his patrons. It's not with a Second Lieutenant to discuss such matters, but the General was apparently still in shock, having realized that the major and very important strategic operation could have been won, but the chance was missed.

"What do you want it for, Second Lieutenant?"

"I had an unpleasant conversation with Major Linden and his friends at the gala dinner last night," I didn't keep it back, "They were trying to figure out from me in a rather rude way who pushed me into the Academy. I didn't talk to them."

"It was done beautifully, gracefully, but foolishly," the General laughed, "Wait for trouble. Our Academy is regularly attended by ministerial commissions, who love to pry into all sorts of interesting details of the lives of students and professors. They pay special attention to the successes and failures of some of them. Whoever's behind Linden is going to tell these military officials, what and who they should pay the most attention to. You may have been mistaken for a future lobbyist of the competitors. So get ready, Second Lieutenant, to answer awkward questions."

Chapter 4

The holidays at the Academy happened, albeit infrequently, and then I went to Ganymede to clear up the backlog of the Lavroff Weapons Company and to see Inga who had returned at last from her training mission. She categorically refused to leave the army as I thought, but I still had to try to convince her.

Jeff and Stein didn't leave the tech zone of the Academy, and it started to bear fruit. The professor, who looked ten years younger now, seemed to be radiating energy. That's what a really important work and a Purpose, with a capital letter, do with a man.

Lieutenant Jeff was in his native state and frankly enjoyed the process, from which he was sometimes distracted only by... Cadet Yakovleva, that speleologist girl, the distant friend of Inga, with whom I was standing in the office of the Director of the Academy after the entrance exam. Heavy losses among freshmen forced General Shiller to recruit additional cadets, and candidate Yakovleva didn't miss her chance, just like she didn't miss Lieutenant Jeff.

By mid-August, my tired but satisfied team reported that all work had been completed. I've invited General Shiller to our internal acceptance of new developments.

I couldn't help it, 'cause we were going to do our tests at the school range. The General did not miss the opportunity to make the cadets work hard and transformed the tests into a combat drill.

A company of cadets in the third year of the Academy played the role of guards of an important military facility on the planet under attack. My platoon was tasked with capturing this facility with minimal damage. To ensure the most reliable results, we have purchased the combat scanners of latest model produced by the Russian Weapons Concern, and equipped the Goannas of the security company with them.

General Shiller has made himself comfortable in the bunker of the observation post at the range with Jeff and the professor, and I've brought my former training platoon into battle, or rather, Inga was in charge of the platoon, and I was just playing the role of consultant and developer representative.

As a matter of fact, the battle drill was short enough.

In each of our three dropships, we've installed six Electronic Warfare stations of our own design, which were specially, at the level of the construction, developed to work together. To optimize their settings, I specifically purchased one of the most powerful computers, which could be a source of pride not only for the Colonial Institute of Technology, but for any of the capital's universities. This miracle of technique took 18 million rubles, but I didn't regret it, the result paid off all the costs. When we switched on our camouflage for the first time, there was a ringing silence in the hangar of the tech zone, which was broken only ten seconds later by a surprise exclamation 'Oh, oh, my goodness' of one of the technicians assigned to us. The dropship, of course, has not become invisible, but even with a look from ten meters, it turned markedly pale and blurred slightly, losing sharpness of the outline. Standard scanners started to distinguish it at best from two to three kilometers, that is, from a distance, when it is almost always too late to take action. The Goannas underwent a very similar modernization, each of them got two EW stations. We had to work a lot on the armored space suits, but the experience of preparing my gear for the Kapteen practice helped us to get through within a reasonable time frame.

Of course, our imaginary enemies tried not to do anything stupid. They set up a network of remote scanners around the guarded object and set up some kind of security perimeter. In addition, one of the three platoons was patrolling the surrounding area at all times, both on foot and with drones. In general, the third-graders complied fully with the statutory procedure for guarding the facility. But against our new camouflage equipment, these measures have been wholly inadequate. We were detecting enemy scanners much earlier than they were able to respond to our equipment.

The dropships landed Inga's platoon three kilometres from the patrol area, and our guys started moving slowly, seeping between outposts of observation and hiding in the folds of the area from the drones. It's convenient to fight when you spot your opponent at a distance, which is many hundreds of meters more than the adversary can detect you himself.

We concentrated on the departure position, and Inga ordered the dropships to launch the attack. The machines with slightly blurred silhouettes flying above the ground, have reached the point of launching of the missiles never detected. A rocket salvo on targets that don't even see you, it's not a big deal. The enemies became particularly sad when they realized that air defence systems could not even catch the enemy vehicles discovered after firing in their sights.

It ended very quickly. After our rocket salvo, the range computer marked ninety-five percent of the guarding company's manpower and equipment as destroyed or disabled, and they froze with the power off like motionless statues. The surviving Goanna and ten infantrymen were unable to confront the full commando platoon that literally came out of nowhere. I gotta hand it to the third graders, we've had our losses, too. The computer counted three defenders' opponents killed.

That was a pretty good score with a bad state of things like that.

General Shiller invited us to his office. Jeff and the professor and I were comfortably seated at the table opposite the director of the Academy. The General smiled. I haven't seen him in such a good mood in a long time.

"Gentlemen, I sincerely congratulate you," Shiller has begun,"You've done a really amazing thing. If the Commission of the Ministry of Defence doesn't adopt it, I will personally send out to all my former comrades-in-arms now in high office the recording of this battle drill with my comments. I want my graduates to fight in machines like this, and I'm gonna achieve it. "

"Thank you, Lieutenant General, Sir," I was pleased to hear those words from the old warrior, but my smile in response was a little sad, "I'm afraid we may indeed need your help soon enough."

***

We didn't wait for the Commission of the Ministry of Defence to come to us on its own, and we have submitted a request to demonstrate our new weapons samples. We had to wait almost a week for an answer from the Ministry. Ministerial officials told us that the process of agreeing on a testing programme and the composition of the commission was under way. Finally, the military bureaucrats told us that we should arrive on September 5th with men and equipment on Callisto, where the specialized test site of the New Equipment and Weapons Commission of the Ministry of Defense was located.

India once tried to develop Jupiter's second largest satellite, but either the Indians didn't have the resources, or they just didn't want to, but they didn't complete the terraforming. As a result, the satellite had a low-powered sun, still hanging over the colony's main city, and an equally weak gravity compensator, which did not cover the entire satellite. As a result, less than a fifth of the surface was habitable. Closer to the boundaries of the inhabited area, conditions were already blatantly lousy, and practically no one lived there, but the giant automated plants and the vast test site of the Ministry of Defence felt good.

The committee puzzled me. The Chairman was General of the Army Barrington, not particularly famous for his military achievements, but known for having been able to organize in the chaos of the war with the quargs service of the rear, transport logistics and troop supply at such level, that this partially compensated for the blatant weakness of the human combat units compared to the quargs who invaded space developed by humans. Well, he was a highly respected military specialist from all points of view.

But the members of the Commission, who I understand represented the military industry, raised a lot of questions. Despite their high ranks, neither Jeff nor I have ever heard of them before, no clear information about them could be found on the network either. The qualification tabs of these gentlemen barely reached the minimum requirements in combat experience, and something told me that they were being pulled by all possible means.

However, there was no choice, and it was hoped that Barrington's presidency would lend some objectivity to the Commission's findings. True, the old General who started the war being far from a young man has now given up a lot, and it was hard to tell what he would do under pressure from the other members of the commission.

Compared to General Shiller's battle drill, the work of the Commission of the Ministry of Defence was much more academic. First the dropships, the Goannas and the commandos in the armored space suits were scanned from different distances, stationary and in motion, simply moving and firing with a standard weapon. All results have been meticulously recorded, and only after that we moved on to the test in close to combat conditions.

Since we indicated in the application that our EW stations not only reduce the visibility of dropships, robots and soldiers in armored space suits, but also allow for new landing tactics, this part of the test programme was extended to two stages. First we simulated a standard landing operation where the dropships entered the atmosphere, approached the landing point, launched thermobaric rockets, touched down and landed commandos. We were naturally irradiated by surface scanners, and when the landing force was detected, our dropships were fired by simulators of light surface-to-air missiles. According to the legend of the tests after the suppression of heavy anti-space defenses of the enemy by an orbital impact the enemy had time to move two platoons of light robots like the Small Dragon to the landing point. Quite a life situation, by the way.

When General Barrington gave us these terms and asked us if we had any questions, I took the floor.

"General of the Army, Sir, before presenting our work to the Commission of the Ministry of Defense, we've run comprehensive in-house tests on our new equipment, and I can say with certainty, that the Commission's proposed test conditions will not allow us to demonstrate to you all its possibilities. I'm asking you to complicate the terms by changing the legend as follows: the orbital strike reached the target only partially. A functioning stationary scanner and a battery of heavy surface-to-air missiles have been retained in the drop zone. In addition, the enemy was able to move a full company of Small Dragons to the threatened area."

The puzzled General hemmed.

"Well, look, Mr Lavroff," now the General spoke to me not as a Second Lieutenant, but as the director of the Lavroff Weapons Company, "You said so yourself, you can't go back. We'll need about 30 minutes to reequip the test site. Get ready."

We were falling into Callisto's thin atmosphere from a low orbit. The dropship with Inga and me was the first to go. The General was a little surprised that I wanted to personally participate in the tests, but there was no objection from him. We turned the EW stations on right away, since there was no reason to save energy. It was possible not to worry at all until the point of probable detection of the standard dropship by a stationary scanner. It was not the Academy, and the instructors weren't going to make any booby traps.

At 30 kilometers above the surface, the dropship computer alerted us with a tonal signal of high radiation intensity by a stationary scanner. For a standard dropship, this meant an 80% probability of detection. We haven't yet been seen, though. After descending another ten kilometers, Inga ordered the dropships to release the EW missile stations. Six low-speed missiles flying in circles around three dropships and keeping them from detection have been added to our machines' substantial cloaking umbrella, we haven't seen anything down there, either. It's easier to camouflage ground targets than air targets.

From an altitude of 15 kilometers, Inga launched disposable rocket drones, which rushed forward to scout the landing site. Ten seconds later, ground targets were glowing red on our tactical projections. We were finally spotted, too. Still, a stationary scanner is a pretty stubborn thing. It was at this point that all three of our dropships fired a coordinated salvo of mock thermobaric rockets, and at the same time, they released two imitators each, which immediately began to act intensively as dropships.

The battery of heavy surface-to-air missiles did not fire. There was no way it's homing-guidance system could capture the slipping markings of the enemy's machines, but the scanners showed six clear marks created by our simulators, and the computer ordered the fire. Twelve missiles darted off the tracks and headed for the sky. Ten Small Dragons fired almost simultaneously, launching 20 more light missiles. The loading machines rolled up to the robots and started feeding new ammunition to their guides, but at that moment our volley reached the surface. 120 unguided thermobaric rockets left the enemy with very little chance.

Only the armored cap of the stationary air-defence emplacement and the pair of Small Dragons which were on the periphery of the drop zone, managed to survive.

Heavy missiles annihilated the simulators, as expected. There were no real explosions, of course, we saw only bright flashes, as there were mock charges in the missile heads, but the test site computer tagged the simulators as destroyed targets.

There were still a lot of missiles flying at us. With no clearly visible targets, they continued flying in our direction, and there was nothing left for their electronic brains to do but order the heads explosion in an area where we might be. That was a shot in the dark. But they were lucky. The exploded heavy rocket warhead bestrewed the second squad dropship with mock strike elements. Luckily, the blast happened about a hundred meters away from the dropship, otherwise we would have missed a third part of the platoon.

"The Dropship-2 sustained damage," the synthesized voice of the test site computer sounded in the cockpit of our machine, "Engine power's down thirty percent. Both thermobaric rocket launchers and the aircraft cannon have been disabled."

It didn't matter anymore. Platoon came in to land. The sluggish and inaccurate fire of the surviving Dragons was answered by a concerted salvo of the dropships aircraft cannons, and then the whole platoon rushed to attack on the lowered ramps. This time the losses were avoided. Inga learned from previous trials, and our Goannas, taking their time, suppressed enemy by fire from afar. We have captured the stationary air-defence battery without a fight. There was no one left to defend it.

The second stage of the test was done according to our scenario. Under the same initial conditions, we chose a completely different tactic, the same one we showed General Shiller. The dropships have landed the commandos outside the stationary scanner area, and the platoon struck from the ground at the same time as the rocket salvo of the dropships. The enemy didn't even have time to fire. A few unaimed shots in our direction didn't count. We've captured the air-defense battery with the missiles on the guides. The battery had no one to shoot at. The stationary scanner was only able to detect the dropships when the thermobaric rockets were being launched, and the battery homing-guidance systems were unable to capture the targets.

When we returned to the operational room of the test site, General Barrington greeted us with a smile, and the faces of his aides looked extremely sour.

"Congratulations, Mr Lavroff," said the General, extending his hand. To me! To a rookie, Second Lieutenant! "You did a great job on a complicated case. I was wrong to doubt you. I think your product will be adopted in no time. We need machines like this now. What do you think, Officers, Sirs?" - He turned to his entourage.

"Ehmm..., General of the Army, Sir," took the floor a short balding man with a slimy look on his face and the shoulder straps of Lieutenant General, "The result, of course, is impressive, but before you make a decision about adopting these samples for military use, It is necessary to consider not only the technical characteristics of the machines and equipment presented to us. The price, the resource intensity of production and the ability of the equipment to withstand the harsh conditions of combat work play an important role. The price of the serial machines promised by the Lavroff Weapons Company exceeds the current price by almost 40%. It's too much."

"But they are vastly superior to standard machines!" - The General was outraged. "Where we used to need a full company, we now have one platoon. This clearly pays off the increase in price and resources."

"Perhaps, General of the Army, Sir, quite possibly. But there is also resistance to breakdowns and failures in combat. This point needs to be clarified," a second Lieutenant General intervened. "In my view, a final decision requires combat tests."

"That's right, General of the Army, Sir," confirmed the second member of the Commission, "We can't adopt raw machines."

"Well, gentlemen," pronounced Barrington with doubt, "If you're so unanimous, we'll schedule battle tests. Any idea where they might be held?"

"Gliese-338, General of the Army, Sir," responded the bald General almost at once, "A few days ago, our drone scout intercepted a signal from one of the major peripheral asteroids. The system has recently been captured by the enemy and there are still settlements on the outskirts. In this case, this is our science station that was doing important research. Important enough for the General Staff to worry about saving them. Except only light scouts can get to it, but quargs have landed on the asteroid. There's not many of them, but the scouts can't do it. The Lavroff Weapons Company is positioning camouflage as the main advantage of its combat vehicles. Hence, they can handle it. It's necessary to land, clear forcefully the entrance to the underground lab and evacuate the personnel. There's only 15 people in there. They'll fit into dropships."

"Isn't it a bit too much for combat trials?" - pronounced Barrington doubtfully, "it's an operation for well-trained special forces."

"It's just right, General of the Army, Sir, especially if the Lavroff Weapons Company can prepare two or three more dropships. Then it'll be totally enough."

I really wanted to smash something on that bastard's head, but I looked calm and waited for the chairman of the Commission to decide.

He was thinking for a minute, and then he turned to me and asked:

"Mr Lavroff, you have entrusted controlling your equipment to a platoon of cadets of the Planetary Commando Academy. Are you that sure about them?"

"I fought with these men on Leiten-5, General of the Army, Sir. If they didn't let me down there…"

"I get it. Are they going to the battle trials, too?"

"If it's authorized by the Director of the Academy, Lieutenant General Shiller."

"In his decision, I have no doubt," Barrington grinned, "Who would you like to see as commander of the operation?"

"Myself, General of the Army, Sir."

"Is that how?" - General raised his eyebrow, "It's the first time I see a head of a weapons company willing to personally lead a combat test of his equipment. Well, in that case, I'll expect you to have the operation plan by tonight. The Ministry of Defence assumes all the costs of its preparation, including the purchase of necessary equipment and ammunition."

Both Lieutenant Generals winced synchronously. Well, I believe, you won't really fall to pieces, Officers, Sirs. And now I'll have enough money to prepare a couple more dropships, maybe three.

***

Barrington gave us not only money, but also a team of qualified engineers and technicians. It was necessary to hurry, the quargs could at any moment find scientists hidden in the underground laboratory, but I shouldn't have gone there with the insufficient forces.

Lieutenant General Shiller gritted his teeth and expressed himself strongly in German. He's already had enough cadet losses, and this operation was likely to increase them significantly, but he didn't even think to refuse me. On the contrary, he did everything to help us. In addition to my former platoon, I've brought with me a platoon of Stephen Fulton. He had already left the hospital and was back at the Academy. After Leiten-5, my relationship with him finally came back to normal, and Stephen himself has been changed a lot by that operation and the serious injury.

I also asked General Barrington to make Captain André Mbia and five or seven of his men available to me. I strongly suspected the services of the recon professionals would come in handy.

"What about your chain of command, Mr Lavroff?" the General was slightly astonished, "You are Second Lieutenant, and Captain Mbia…" the General fell silent and looked on his tablet, "No, not a captain, he's already Major Mbia, to put it mildly, outranks you."

"We'll make a deal, General of the Army, Sir. Major Mbia has fought before under my command, he was a captain back then, and I was a cadet, but that doesn't change things."

"You got a facetious biography, Mr Lavroff," General laughed,"I'll find out where the Major is now and I'll make arrangements."

***

Despite all the help and constant stimulating kicks from above, we were able to leave for Gliese system only three days later. However, reconnaissance probes regularly sent to the asteroid area confirmed that the laboratory had not yet been detected by the enemy. Anyway, the situation could change at any second, and we would have to fly about ten days.

To an empty point of space, one jump from Gliese, we arrived on a medium landing transport. There were already three medium-size reconnaissance ships waiting for us, according to Barrington, they were equipped with the most advanced systems of camouflage, as the Earth Federation currently possessed. I was very sorry I didn't get a chance to work with their EW stations before the operation, but now it was too late to think about it, and no one would have let me do it, anyway.

According to the approved plan, we were to load two dropships into each of the recon ships. This operation proved to be quite non-trivial, as the recon ships were never intended to carry commandos. Technically, the interior holds were sufficient, but a complete lack of the necessary infrastructure, such as special grabs and restraints, as well as launch catapults to release dropships into space, created a lot of unexpected difficulties that had to be solved on the spot.

Mbia and his men arrived here before us, and we met in a tiny chief cabin of our small squadron's flagship, and Lieutenant Commander Yoon Gao was shocked by the failure of the chain of command. Yoon Gao, who was the same rank as Mbia, was expecting a full report from the Second Lieutenant, however, when I walked into the cabin, I couldn't even open my mouth, as Major Mbia jumped up and, with a smile on his black face, shouted:

"Second Lieutenant, Sir, Major Mbia and seven scouts from the 3rd Regiment of the 105th Infantry Division have arrived at your disposal."

To be honest, I didn't see that coming, but tried to get out of this unorthodox situation, while not putting Yoon Gao completely out of his mind. "I'm glad to see you again, Major, Sir," I responded, saluting Mbia and shaking his hand, then turned to the ship's commander and continued, "Lieutenant Commander, Sir, Second Lieutenant Lavroff has arrived with two platoons of commandos to conduct a joint rescue operation."

"Yoon," having difficulty to hold back his laughter, Mbia tried to lift the captain of the ship out of shock, "I'm sorry I didn't warn you right away. I only command my men here. The Second Lieutenant is in charge of the operation."

"You could have told me right away," a Chinese man recovered with an angry look at Mbia, "what for is this circus of Guizhou here... Nice to meet you, Second Lieutenant. Sit down, let's discuss the details of your delivery to the location and the landing procedure."

***

The asteroid that was our target was a pretty big planetoid. It had no atmosphere of its own, but was large enough to form into an almost regular ball. This pile of ice and stone formed on the periphery of the star Gliese system at the time of planetary formation, but never became a real planet, unable to clear its orbit with its own gravity from the rocks and debris that make up the analogue of the Kuiper belt.

The reconnaissance ships did not venture deep into the system. Each day the quargs increased the density of the network of watchbeacons and patrols, and Lieutenant Commander Gao considered it too dangerous to go directly to the target of the operation. Considering that the quargs at the Gliese assault surprised us with their new developments in the field of camouflage, I could not disagree. If the adversary has improved the means of ensuring obscurity, he may have advanced in the scanning systems as well, so none of us wanted to risk it.

10,000,000 kilometers from the target, the outer flaps of the hold gate opened, and improvised pneumatic catapults smoothly pushed the dropships into outer space. Having waited a minute for the dropships to move away from the ships at a safe distance, Yoon Gao gave the order to begin the careful diminishing airspeed and course change. The ships were to turn on a wide arc and to leave the system again, and then three days later to return to the rendezvous point and pick up the dropships.

"Good luck, commandos!" We got a short message on the laser-optic channel, and the comms went dead. The ships disappeared among the lights of the distant stars, and our machines continued their flight by inertia towards the target.

It would take us almost 28 hours to get to the surface of the asteroid. I thought we'd rather have some tedious time in the dropships poorly-equipped for long flights, under safe cover of our new EW stations, than go on more comfortable ships closer to the target, but with questionable results.

Seven hours later, our scanners picked up an encrypted pulse signal from the asteroid. Scientists have confirmed they're fine for now. We naturally had the exact location of the laboratory and a detailed map of the surrounding area, but the data on the quarg forces we had was approximate. Reconnaissance believed that the quargs had deployed on the asteroid no more than a standard infantry company.

In preparation for the operation, we had to replace almost all the ammunition and reconfigure some of the equipment. Landing on an asteroid with no atmosphere and very low gravity is not a trivial task. For example, the thermobaric warheads that dropships normally carry will not work under these conditions, because they need an atmosphere that contains a lot of oxygen. Movement on the surface at low gravity also creates difficulties for the unaccustomed person. We've trained under these conditions, of course, but I can't say that there have been many such exercises.

But low gravity had one huge plus that we planned to use. Dropships cannot take off the planets, and they are brought back into orbit by special transports, but not in this case. The gravity of the asteroid, negligible compared to the planetary, was not an obstacle to dropship engines. We could go into outer space on our own, without the help of ships.

As we approached our goal relatively slowly, I had time to reflect and even scold myself for not having done the scanner upgrades, because I wanted to see the enemy's locations as soon as possible. But on balance, I have come to the conclusion that we just did not have neither resources nor the time to do it, so now all we have to hope for is our advanced camouflage.

There's a long-standing law of villainy: if something bad may happen, it will happen for sure. A special case of this law is well known in the form of the 'law of sandwich', which always falls on the floor by the buttered side down.

Another special case of the aforementioned law was waiting for us down on the surface of the asteroid: the quargs were hanging out in the immediate vicinity of the lab entrance, and there were an awful lot of them.

"Staff Sergeant Fulton," I called the Second Platoon Commander.

"Here, Commander."

"Set aside two dropships for the distraction. The third squad will be under my command. Take the coordinates of the drop point. Your task is to pull back the enemy's forces and tie them up by combat for 30 minutes. I forbid you to engage in a close combat. Take advantage of our EW systems and stay at the maximum range of effective fire. Is the task clear?"

"That's right, Commander."

"Thirty minutes after landing, break off the enemy, load into your dropships and go into outer space. Move to the rendezvous point yourself."

"Got it. Your permission to fulfill?"

"Do it. Good luck, Stephen."

"Thank you, Commander."

"First platoon and third squad of the second platoon start diminishing airspeed. Fulton should attack ten minutes ahead of us."

Inga and com-3 of the 2nd Platoon have confirmed that they have accepted the order, and I turned my attention to tactical projection.

Now the dropships of the two squads of Fulton's platoon have moved forward and slightly corrected their course. I gave them the task of making a noise 200 kilometers from the lab, but I wasn't sure that all the quargs would come to this noise.

Below us, on the surface of the asteroid were the units of the full infantry battalion of the enemy, reinforced by two heavy robots, which looked like the Mammoths. Away from the main forces sat on the ground landing transport, which must have brought here this friendly staff.

I started thinking. If the diversion draws insufficient quarg forces from the entrance to the lab, the task will be extremely difficult. The scientists in the bunker already knew about us. Laser-optical transmission is almost impossible to intercept or jam, but the receiver needs to be in direct view, and its exact location needs to be known. We knew the location, so the lab residents, wearing their space suits, were waiting in the airlock for our command to get out. Of course, they only had civilian space suits, no armour, no weapons, which were unable to withstand even the impact of fragments and bullets from light hand weapons, so I had to provide a few safe minutes at the entrance to the lab to load the scientists into the dropship. We were minutes away from the active phase of the operation. A decision had to be made right now.

"Third squads of first and second platoons to change course. Your mission is to attack the enemy landing transport with unguided rockets from a distance of 30 kilometres, then to land and start a demonstrative shooting towards the enemy. Don't get too close. Just mark the attack and head straight back to the dropships and into space. Move to the rendezvous point yourself. Cadet Jaswinder commands your team."

"Got it," the squad commanders responded in chorus.

The quargs are bound to react painfully to an attack on the transport ship. There's a high probability of the battalion headquarters on its board, and a commander is almost a god for a quarg. It was to be hoped that a simultaneous attack in two locations would force the enemy to expose the space that seemed safe.

Fulton was the first to start. He conducted the rocket salvo as on a test site, seeing the targets perfectly, but remaining invisible to them. The quargs, however, proved to be experienced warriors, and the effect of surprise lasted no more than 20 seconds from that moment, when whithin the enemy battle formation the fountains of explosions of warheads were raised. The response salvo was sluggish and inaccurate, which was not surprising as it was impossible to capture the targets properly by the fire control systems, but the fact that it followed so quickly did not please me.

What does an experienced soldier do when he realizes his fire doesn't reach the enemy, armed with longer-range weapons or simply well-disguised? He either retreats, hides and calls for reinforcements or artillery fire, or shortens the distance by thrust and engages in a close combat. The quargs never liked to retreat, but they didn't forget to call for reinforcements. The enemy platoon, which was thinned out after the rocket strike, moved towards Fulton's position.

Stephen didn't get too heroic. In strict compliance with the order, he retreated, keeping his distance, and showered the enemy with anti-tank missiles of his Goannas. Despite the Small Dragons' pilots evident high skill, after a few minutes, all three of the enemy's robots stood still amid rocks and ice blocks.

The quarg infantry were reluctant to pursue the enemy, who turned out to be very aggressive, without support, but there was already a company of quargs and both heavy robots rushing to the battlefield. Low gravity allowed them to move very quickly, making giant jumps above the surface. Once again, I noted with dismay the enemy's high level of training. It was felt that this battalion was very good at fighting in such conditions. I had no direct contact with Fulton, so I could neither help him nor warn him of the danger, and I could only hope for the fighting skill of my former enemy.

The attack on the quarg transport ship began with a rocket salvo. 80 high-explosive warheads lay in the immediate vicinity or exploded directly on the hull of the enemy ship. Of course, they couldn't penetrate the armor. I am not sure that even if the warheads of the rockets were cumulative, we would have succeeded. After all, the ship's armor is designed for space combat where much bigger calibres are used. However, the ship was completely unprepared for this development. Its main hold was open, landing ramp on the ground, and my cadets had the good sense to attack from the right side. As a result, several rockets flew inside the ship and exploded there. They still couldn't do any fatal damage to the transport ship, but the very fact of the attack and the unfortunate unexpected losses caused the enemy to rage.

The Mammoths who were making huge leaps towards the Fulton platoon, changed direction abruptly to almost the opposite and rushed to eliminate the new threat. All of the enemy forces not yet engaged in the battle were on the move and began to converge towards the transport ship. A few minutes later, when the battle broke out on the approach to the enemy ship, I gave the order to launch the rescue operation.

The quargs have not resisted our landing. So far, they've had far more interesting affairs. I was very worried about the units that attacked the ship. There's an enemy force out there that's gonna be hard to break off, and a frontal collision at this correlation of forces, my men can't take it. Nevertheless, I had a specific task ahead of me, and I focused on it.

The two squads of the first platoon with enviable agility formed a defensive perimeter around the entrance to the laboratory.

"Major Mbia, I need a temporary electronic perimeter, high-altitude remote scanners and drones over the drop zone."

"Got it, Commander."

The entrance hatch, disguised as a piece of rock, trembled and moved away. People in civilian space suits started to pop out in the slit. Bent under the weight of the voluminous briefcases, they rushed to the nearest dropship, accompanied by commandos in armor.

Whether the quargs had a bright head who understood, that an attack conducted by such small forces, is nothing but a distraction, whether their scanners found the entrance to the shelter and the people in civilian suits without any camouflage equipment, but Inga's anxious voice was heard in my helmet:

"Commander! Two Mammoths, four Small Dragons and a platoon of enemy infantry heading here. They do not see us yet. I'm picking up missile launches!"

"Everybody, away from the bunker! We don't have more than 15 seconds! Dropships take off now!" I screamed on the command frequency and put my machine's engines on a fast track.

Good thing the scientists were already on board. If the quargs had come to their senses thirty seconds earlier, we'd have very serious problems, although I wouldn't call them trivial anyway. Both Mammoths fired missiles from 50 kilometers. They hit the squares. They haven't spotted our landing party, but by opening the entrance, the lab has unmasked itself, and now the quargs had a clearly visible target.

We almost did it. The heavy assault robot Mammoth is a terrible weapon. I personally checked it out sitting in its cockpit and shooting quargs on Leiten-5. Now I was on the other side of the sighting device.

The plan was to blow up the lab before leaving the asteroid. I guess now it was no longer necessary. The surface of the planetoid in the impact zone exploded, throwing upward the titanic sultans of stone and ice crumbs, which rose to unrealistic heights because of low gravity. We've been hit by the edge of this man-made eruption. If there was an atmosphere, the shock wave would have caused a lot of trouble, but even so, part of the platoon was hit by the hail of shrapnel and striking elements.

On the tactical projection, the loss of telemetry data from five commandos' space suits and one Goanna has been marked with red light. The dropship of the second squad has been damaged, and its camouflage deteriorated, but by the second it was getting more and more re-established, nearing the norm - the dropship's computer used our latest software algorithm and gradually introduced corrections to the settings of EW stations, taking into account the changes caused by the damage.

I realized that they wouldn't let us get into our dropships and leave the asteroid. We had to do something about the Mammoths, or in a few minutes, they'll grind us to dust.

"Inga, slowly pull the platoon here," I indicated the assembly point on the tactical projection.

"Dropship-2, do as I do."

"Yes, Sir," the pilot of the second machine responded immediately.

We flew along a great arc, pressing ourselves to the surface and covering ourselves with EW stations, that were running at full capacity, from the Mammoths and Dragons' scanners. Fulton was still fighting. According to the order, he had to last about ten minutes. I was very concerned that the fighting in the area of the quarg transport ship was still going on. One of the surviving drones suspended just outside our drop site, detected gunfire flares and explosions in that direction.

A few minutes later, we went into the rear of the quargs, which were chasing excitedly the first platoon. Inga has almost reached the rendezvous point I indicated. The dropship's sighting and navigation complex confidently captured the enemy's heavy robots and reported readiness to fire.

"Dropship-2, ready to fire?"

"Ready!"

"Fire the salvo!"

Eighty unguided rockets left the launchers and darted for the targets, and we, without waiting for results, drastically changed course and, continuing almost to scratch the surface by the bottom, flew to the assembly point at maximum possible speed to pick up the first platoon. I didn't expect to destroy the Mamonts with our missiles. Those armored carcasses are way out of their league, but our evil gifts may well have knocked down the outer sensors of scanners, cracked the attached implements, and thereby dramatically reduce the fighting efficiency of the giants and their firing accuracy.

When we descended to the surface at the rendezvous point, twelve cadets in armoured space suits and one Goanna climbed the dropship ramp. Major Mbia's men did not participate in the battle and escaped with one wounded man, and we lost almost half of our troops, even though I still don't know the losses of Fulton and the units that attacked the enemy ship. Someone in the capital will pay dearly for this, even if not immediately. I do not forgive it.

We took off from the asteroid and started to accelerate slowly. Compared to the spacecraft's engines, our weak engines could not give us such a formidable acceleration, and it took us almost 48 hours to reach the rendezvous point with the reconnaissance ships. The Fulton platoon was waiting for us there. Stephen managed to avoid casualties. Jaswinder's squads' attack on the quarg ship distracted most of the pursuers from Fulton, so he led a few, not-so-persistent enemies through the icy desert, then he broke away from them and went into space.

The recon ships arrived on time. I've ordered everyone to board, and the ships went out of the system for another 48 hours, and Inga and I at our dropship stayed to wait for Jaswinder's squad at the rendezvous point.

We saw quarg patrols, but they flew far enough so we wouldn't be afraid to be detected in our immobile and well-camouflaged machine. Twenty-four hours went by, and I decided to do some reconnaissance, heading in the direction of the asteroid. Inga shrugged her shoulders and said she already wanted to suggest it.

We took the risk of launching a drone scout, which sped up and went passively, without active scanning, a few hundred kilometers from the asteroid and then returned to our dropship. After analyzing the imagery obtained by the probe, the dropship's computer identified the wreckage of the dropship of squad 3 of Fulton Platoon.

It was still unclear where Jaswinder's dropship went. We were on our way back to the rendezvous point. We were flying not directly, but along an expanding spiral, and avoided meeting with the quargs, who were increasing their presence in the system. We scanned the space for our comrades, but only by taking the risk, and by maximizing the scanning power, did we find a weak mark far away from the rendezvous point. The dropship of squad 3 of the first platoon looked terrible. It was pierced all over by striking elements of enemy warheads like a hedgehog, but the camouflage was almost normal, which saved the machine from detection by the quargs. The power plant was running at about a quarter capacity, and the dropship itself was overloaded, because it carried now two squads. One Goanna had to be abandoned and blown up, but the cadets removed from the planetoid all the living and six dead comrades.

We barely made it to the rendezvous point, but we still did, and the commander of the three medium scouts, Yoon Gao, with obvious relief ordered a course leading away from the Gliese-338 system.

A few hours after we left the system, a grim Mbia came up to me and said he had a serious conversation with me.

"Commander," the Major started talking with some hesitation in his voice, as if doubting whether he should ask such a question, but nevertheless decided, "Do you have any powerful enemies?"

"Not without it, André, not without it," I answered in an unhappy voice, "and what gave you that idea?"

"I thought so," said the Major, slightly nodding his head, "The thing is, Commander, when you ordered me to control the area, adjacent to the drop zone, I came across the remains of a network of recon drones. Someone sent them there before the quargs arrived, then, of course, the enemy found and destroyed most of the devices, but there was something left. I took the information off them because there was no special cipher used except that of the Army. Now, when you were here on board the ship, you told us that, according to the recon data, there was no more than a standard quarg company on the asteroid. You were relying on intelligence provided by the General Staff, weren't you?"

"Naturally, I was."

"Now, this intel is fake. It's not a mistake, it's not inaccuracy, it's a forgery. The thing is, the asteroid was scouted by the Eel-3MU probes. I know this model well. Such a probe accelerates, activates the EW station, and travels tangentially to the reconnaissance object, scanning the space. The sensitivity of its scanners is more than enough to pick up signals of the recon drones from the surface, it must have picked them, sent them back the key code and received the information pack. And I got the same pack, when I found the remains of a network of drones on the surface. And I want to tell you, Commander, that from the very beginning, from the time the quargs landed, there was a battalion reinforced by heavy robots on the asteroid, and not a standard enemy company at all. Someone purposely distorted the probe's data, and that someone obviously didn't want you and your people coming back alive."

"Thank you, André," I answered almost a minute later, "that's a very valuable information for me. I knew I had enemies, but I didn't think they'd do something like this. Please forgive me for unwittingly putting you and your people at such risk."

"No need, Commander," Mbya grinned, "We're sorry about those killed, they were real soldiers, but we're still alive. And you know what... If you ever make it to a free ticket for a party like this, don't forget to bring a ticket for me."

"In fact, André," in return I smiled with no joy, "in the future I plan to organize parties of this kind myself, and not get free tickets. And you can rest assured, as soon as I do, I will send you a VIP invitation to the front-row table, closer to the stage."

***

Back to Ganymede, we were taken by the same transport ship that brought us to the Gliese system.

General Shiller already knew the results of our raid, and immediately upon arrival, Major Mbia and I were received in his office.

"The fact that you are alive, officers," - Schiller said after the reciprocal greetings, "is a real surprise to those who know. It's that you've accomplished a task in that scenario, that few people believe at all."

"We lost 14 men, Lieutenant General," I responded. "When I left for the operation, I promised you I'd keep your people safe. Unfortunately, I failed, and I didn't keep my promises."

"This is a war, Second Lieutenant, I've told you many times before. Everyone who went with you volunteered. I had no right to send cadets to such an operation just by my order."

"Lieutenant General, Sir," said Major Mbia in low voice, "It's not just about the war and the inevitable losses. We've been betrayed."

"Betrayed? What do you mean, Major? Quargs don't make contact with people. How could you be betrayed?"

"It wasn't in the reports, Lieutenant General, Sir, I didn't want this information to fall into the wrong hands early," I answered for Mbia, "André, tell the Lieutenant General everything I heard from you right after the operation."

Shiller listened silently, without interrupting or asking questions. With every word the Major has said, the General has become increasingly gloomy.

"For you, Second Lieutenant, that only means one thing," said the General after Mbia had finished his report, "Now these people are going to stop at nothing. They've got nowhere else to go. You still have some time until they know that you have evidence of betrayal, but as soon as they realize they're in danger of being exposed…"

"But, Lieutenant General…"

"Put aside the ranks, Major."

"Yes, Sir. But we don't know who did it."

"With this evidence base, the Feds are gonna run this case in no time, rest assured," the General grinned with no joy, "You have no idea what these guys are capable of after the 'Go!' command. So I suggest you hold that information for now. You'll feel safer."

Chapter 5

In order to pronounce the decision of the Commission, General of the Army Barrington formally invited me to the central building of the Ministry of Defense, that was situated in the suburbs of the capital. I left my fly-car at the departmental area, where I was met by a lieutenant in security uniform who escorted me to the office of the Chairman of the Commission on New Technology and Armaments.

Barrington wasn't alone in his office.

There was another high-ranking officer with the Major General's shoulder straps sitting at the conference table, looking like anyone but the military. The uniform sat on him like a saddle on a cow, and it immediately felt like he was wearing it very rarely.

"General of the Army, Sir..." I began my report, but the General stopped me with a gesture of hand.

"Good afternoon, Mr Lavroff, you're not here as a Second Lieutenant, you're here as the head of the Lavroff Weapons Company, so feel free. Sit down. Before we get down to business, there's someone I'd like you to meet. In fact, you've already met, except the circumstances of your meeting didn't allow for small talk or even a simple introduction. Major General, Sir, I'd like to introduce to you the officer who organized and personally led your evacuation from the Gliese system. Second Lieutenant Igor Lavroff, who is also the head of the Lavroff Weapons Company."

"It's a pleasure, young man," the Major General said it completely unmilitarylike, "I am professor Suparman Alatas, Indonesian Military Technical University in Jakarta. In the Gliese system, I was the head of the Science Laboratory that made researches… "

The professor was silenced by Barrington's hard gaze, "but it doesn't matter. It's important that my people and I are very grateful to you for saving us."

I really didn't get to meet the scientists that were rescued. They weren't flying in my dropship to the rendezvous point, and there they were immediately transferred to one of the recon ships, and it left the system without delay.

"Always happy to help, Mr Alatas," I have taken a free form of communication.

"So, gentlemen, to the main theme of our meeting," pronounced Barrington in official tone, "Combat tests of the new EW systems for dropships, combat robots and armored space suits, developed by the Lavroff Weapons Company were considered successful by the Commission. The Ministry of Defence has decided to adopt these systems and to place an order to upgrade 1,000 dropships and the corresponding number of Goanna-2M combat robots and armored space suits. Upon completion of this order, the Ministry will decide to place orders for similar modernization of other weapons and equipment. Formally, the order must be placed through a public competition, but since there were no applications to participate in it from anyone other than the Lavroff Weapons Company, it was decided to conclude the contract with it. Congratulations, Mr. Lavroff, on your first state contract. That's a great thing to acquire."

"Thank you, General of the Army, Sir," I replied, still ignoring the requirements of the army regulations. However, the General did not insist.

"And now, gentlemen, the most interesting thing to begin," Barrington grinned, "discussion on the terms of the contract. The Lavroff Weapons Company gave us a price in the primary documentation provided for the tests, and that price suited the Ministry. But the terms of payment still need to be discussed. The contract provides for an advance for the purchase of equipment and supplies and other necessary expenses, which will be transferred to the account of the Lavroff Weapons Company as soon as the contract is concluded. The issue is the amount of this advance. I'm waiting for you, Mr. Lavroff, to justify the amount."

Yes, it was a key issue for me. I knew exactly how much money I needed to fulfill the contract. We've already calculated all this with Jeff and Professor Stein, but I wanted to get a much larger advance from the Ministry to spend it on our next development.

"General of the Army, Sir," I started to carefully formulate my idea, "The Commission you presided over was able to make sure that the Lavroff Weapons Company is able to offer our armed forces truly breakthrough technology. However, considerable resources are required for their development and, above all, for reaching practical results and creation of functioning models. We are not asking the State to fund our research. We are a private company, and I understand that no one will give us the funds for these purposes, but I do hope that the Ministry will find it possible to increase the advance on this contract. This will allow us to present to your Commission one or two more of our developments by the end of the state-commissioned work, which will be as breakthrough as the new EW complex."

"I thought it might come up," nodded the General, "and that's another reason why I invited Professor Alatas to our meeting today. Now, gentlemen, I'll leave you for about an hour, I have another appointment. In that time, Mr Lavroff, you need to convince the distinguished professor that your new developments might actually be of interest to the Ministry of Defense. It's up to you entirely to provide the amount of the advance needed by your company that will eventually be specified in the contract. Come, gentlemen, my assistant will escort you to the office where you are comfortable."

The Indonesian professor turned out to be a very passionate man. The physics of plasma, which was his main specialization, required extensive knowledge in related fields, and the professor possessed all this knowledge and even more.

I, of course, did not reveal all the cards to the professor, but I shared with him the basics of our, or rather my, groundwork from the past life. I outlined the plans for new scanners and communications and the principles on which these developments are based, and hinted that the level to which we plan to take our devices will allow us to overcome the current imbalance that both we and the adversaries had now: the predominance of the means of electronic warfare over the means of communication. In my past history, there was also a similar period, and I knew exactly how this problem was solved.

The hour passed unnoticed, and Barrington's polite aide invited us back to the General's office.

"So, Professor, what do you think of Mr Lavroff's plans?" - asked Barrington with interest. The General looked cheerful and energetic. Apparently, the meeting didn't spoil his mood.

"You know, Vincent," wistfully responded the professor, naming the General by his first name and by so doing, disregarding all the army regulations, but the General did not react, apparently knowing well that the Indonesian is actually not a military man, "If it were up to me to give the money to this young man, he would have gotten everything he asked for, and I'd call him every night and ask him if he needed more."

"Is that what I'm hearing from you, Suparman?" - Barrington looked betrayed in the best of expectations, "I mean, guys usually don't get a penny out of you, That's why I brought you in. I was sure that with your participation no ruble of the budget would be wasted. And here it is! He wanted more..."

"Vincent," responded the professor in low voice, "Mr Lavroff is not just offering us new technical devices or another wonderful gun. What he's capable of doing will give us a real chance to win, and when we look at the situation on the fronts, it's not about getting the victory closer, it's about making it possible."

"Is it that serious?" - The General looked puzzled.

"It's more than that."

"Well, Mr Lavroff, I didn't expect this turn of events. I need to think it over and to work out the details at the Ministry. The decision will be announced to you in the course of the day tomorrow."

We received an advance of 90% of the contract amount. I was afraid even to dream of that. Professor Alatas and General Barrington, apparently, were able to find the right words to justify this decision.

***

I wasn't too interested in the news, I had enough worries without them, but I couldn't ignore what was happening on the net. There was a huge corruption scandal going on in the Earth Federation, and maybe I would've let it pass by, but my evil intracranial worm of doubt once again grabbed its hammers and began to beat them into the bregma, but he didn't really explain what the catch was. I have decided not to ignore the activity of this useful animal, and tried to understand the problem better.

Upon closer examination, it transpired that the target of the attack was the Russian Weapons Concern. It's been dragged through the mud to the fullest extent by online media, especially those I knew were actively sponsored by Global Weapons Industries. RWC was accused of unfair competition and of bribing officials for creating favourable conditions for the Concern to participate in the competitions of the Ministry of Defense. This song is as old as the world, not only as this one, but as the one where I was the Brigadier General.

After a few days of this campaign, the opponents of RWC went from words to deeds, which has led to the arrest of several high-ranking Concern officials. Maybe there were some real facts behind all that big talk, maybe not, but the usual legal merry-go-round with investigators, lawyers, witnesses, security measures and groups of unidentified persons was starting to spin very smoothly.

As long as it wasn't really about me, I kept doing my own thing. The Academy was time-consuming, I also had to meet regularly with contractors, officials of the Ministry of Defence and other agencies, equipment suppliers and with a host of other people of interest, without whom it would not have been possible to produce a large number of EW complexes.

After receiving generous funding, my engineering team purchased expensive equipment and was immersed in working on new processors based on knowledge from my past life, that was poured into my brain by good Dr Silk. We were seriously committed to fundamentally changing the quality of communications in the Federation Army. I've been thinking about implementing here units of remote-controlled assault drones, led by one pilot in the control module, that became standard in my former world. I haven't shared this idea with anyone yet, but many of the new developments of the Lavroff Weapons Company have somehow worked to translate it into reality. And of course, somewhere in a foggy perspective, I've already distinguished the blurred contours of the hyperportal gate, which was my main task, but before that, local technology had to grow and grow.

Ten days after the completion of our operation, I was suddenly summoned by the Chief of the General Staff Academy to his office. General of the Army O'Sullivan listened to my report with a solemn expression, he handed me a new qualification tab, enriched with some more combat experience, and announced that for the successful raid on the Gliese system, I was presented to the extraordinary rank. So now I've become a lieutenant, and I'm on par with the regular alumni of the academies.

Because of all these concerns, I've only occasionally followed the corruption scandal that was unfolding increasingly, and I guess that's why I didn't hear the alarm bells in the network reporters' speeches, although the first signs of trouble didn't start with them.

The Commission of the Ministry of Defense has arrived at the Academy. I didn't know what those bloated turkeys with the generals' shoulder straps were doing, and I didn't really want to know, until a messenger showed up to our class where we studied interaction between branches of the armed forces and asked me to come out, so that I can appear before the High Commission and answer its questions. As I walked out of the class, I saw the gloating smirks on the faces of Major Linden and his friends, but I decided not to bother and not to make a big deal out of it. Probably for nothing.

Having listened to my report, a Lieutenant General, overfilled with the sense of his own significance, but who didn't deign to introduce himself, told me:

"Lieutenant Lavroff, the Commission has carefully reviewed your personnel file, and we have questions both for you and for your patrons who had recommended you for admission to the General Staff Academy. We'll ask them the relevant questions, and here and now you will answer, Lieutenant."

I waited silently for the continuation. A verbiage like that could have frightened or embarrassed me 50 years ago, and it's not even a fact. The childhood, spent in an orphanage and a cadet school, they, you know, harden man's soul.

"Aren't you curious what the Commission would like to know, Lieutenant?" That was a really stupid qiestion from the Major General to the right of the Chairman of the Commission.

"Major General, Sir," I answered with a straight voice, "I look forward to the Chairman or members of the Commission asking me questions and I'm prepared to give the fullest possible answers. Any other action or words on my part would be a violation of the chain of command."

"All right, Lieutenant, if you want a formal approach, here's your first question," the Chairman of the Commission again took the floor and, looking into the tablet, continued, "How is it that being an ordinary pupil of a nondescript school in Titan, all of a sudden, within a few months, you had four degrees in higher education?"

They tortured me for over two hours. All of these questions, in one form or another, have been asked before, and now I was answering them monotonously, trying to figure out what they really want from me.

Something new only appeared at the very end of this interrogation.

"The Analysis Department of the Ministry of Defence recently received a report from Colonel General Swirsky on the new Gliese-4 battle scenario you applied in the course of the training task. This scenario has achieved combat efficiencies that are more than three times greater than the result achieved in real combat by Lieutenant General Sanders, and more than double the maximum efficiency theoretically calculated by the analysts of the General Staff. The Commission carefully examined the training operation.

We're interested in what you've guided your decision to remove the orbital fortresses and ships of the Seventh Fleet from the defense of the planet and concentrate them to protect a small area of the surface where you and your troops were stationed. Respond, Lieutenant."

"I was primarily motivated by operational effectiveness, Lieutenant General, Sir. In addition, I have taken into account the possibility of giving safe haven to at least part of the planet's population, albeit a small one."

"Were you aware that most of the planet's population would be left unprotected and would fall into enemy hands?"

"Yes, I was aware. This decision was taken consciously."

"Very well, Lieutenant, very well. Now, the last question. You are the head of the Lavroff Weapons Company, which now fulfills the contract on a state order. At the same time, you are being trained at the General Staff Academy in order to become a senior officer of our army. How do you explain that fact?"

"I see no contradiction in these two occupations, Colonel General, Sir. I'm really looking forward to a military career. And I really want to produce the high-quality weapons and military equipment that our army needs."

"Doesn't it seem to you, Lieutenant, that your potential high-ranking position in the Army would be able to help your company gain an advantage over competitors in the Miistry of Defence competitions?"

Something stung my brain. My militant worm must wake up again. I've heard that wording before. Exactly! This is roughly how accusations were made against the functionaries of the Russian Weapons Concern.

"I do not use such concepts as «seems», Colonel General, Sir," I replied calmly, "Any speculation not supported by facts and evidence remains speculation. I can only say in earnest that I have never considered such an opportunity."

"You should have done that, Lieutenant. These things are worth thinking about before others think about them.

You're free to go, Lieutenant, you're still free at the moment, but think at leisure about what I'm saying."

***

Jeff's call caught me at lunch at the Academy.

"Commander, what's going on?" My chief engineer sounded genuinely troubled.

"I don't know yet, Jeff, what's the matter?"

"It's been an hour since the network media has trashed our company. We're being charged with collusion with the Russian Weapons Concern. Some rogues have conducted a journalistic investigation and say with a clever look that we are buying a lot of different equipment from RWC, and are therefore linked with them by economic interests, which means we can participate in corruption schemes as well. I've never heard such nonsense in my life, but they all carry it out to people with spiritual expressions on their faces. Monsterrrs!"

"Well, stop, Jeff. Looks like the GWI boys are on the warpath. We're not their main target, but apparently they think they can solve all their problems with one blow. Call the professor and look for a reliable law firm. We're gonna need a good lawyer."

I should have taken care of it sooner, but better late than never. We had our own legal staff, of course, but they specialized in commercial law, and this was clearly a different bias.

"Commander, if you want speed and reliability, you don't have to look for anyone. My sister's married to a good lawyer. His field of activity is criminal cases. I think this is our case. This kind of information support is not going to happen without an appearance of law enforcement or security personnel."

"All right, Jeff, get in touch with him, we'll figure out a way to get out of this ass."

***

In the comfortable salon of the luxury fly-car, President Tobolsky returned to discussing his current affairs with his assistant, this process had been interrupted by the flight to the commissioning ceremony of the new battleship.

"What's next on the list, Ignat?"

"Mr President, you asked me to let you know if Second Lieutenant Lavroff and his weapons company make something of note."

"So? Has he?"

"As far as I can tell, it worked. They did a pretty good EW complex and even conducted its combat tests in the

Gliese system, successfully evacuated the personnel of the plasma weapons research laboratory."

"Is that how? And by the way, there's some movement on the plasma?"

"So far, it's just basic research. It's a long way from functioning samples."

"Okay, let's get back to Lavroff."

"The Ministry of Defence adopted his EW complex and made a major contract with him."

"Haven't the competitors tried to eat him up yet?"

"They tried, but he refused to sell his company. It is also suspected that his men should have received a very unpleasant surprise during the combat trials, but either something didn't work, or they were successful in getting out of trouble, and the second is more likely. And now there's a serious online information attack on his company. It's being pulled into a RWC scandal. All the charges are clearly false, but everything is done professionally, and public opinion is being shaped accordingly."

"Keep an eye on him. If anything significant happens, report it immediately."

***

I was arrested at the Academy, in my room. There were three officers of the criminal investigation department, they presented an arrest warrant and offered to follow them. They behaved fairly and allowed me to inform my lawyer.

And then it got really crazy. Neither I nor the lawyer could long understand what I was accused of, but when the charge was made, the sense of delusion increased.

"Arrested Lavroff, you are charged with multiple attempts to bribe federal officials for personal gain to create favourable working conditions under the State contract with the Ministry of Defence for your mother's company. In addition, you are charged with misappropriation of funds received by the Lavroff Weaponry Company as an advance on the State contract. Together, these offences are punishable by deprivation of liberty for up to 15 years. Do you plead guilty to these crimes?" - The investigator has silenced, awaiting our reaction.

"My client pleads not guilty to any of the charges and would like to see the evidence, Mr Investigator," pronounced my lawyer Sergei Isaev in a neutral voice. The investigation was unable, by definition, to provide reasonable evidence, but there were no fools in the Earth Federation Security Service, experienced and professional investigators worked here. They were very good at building cases, and they did it with pleasure, especially when they were well motivated. What can be done if there is no direct evidence of corruption? There are several ways.

First, the lack of direct evidence can be compensated by more circumstantial evidence. I was shown endless CCTV footage of me actually meeting various people, some of whom were indeed government officials. A number of recordings were silent, while other recordings contained particular phrases, like 'It seems to me that such an approach would be mutually beneficial' or 'I believe that it is in the interest of both parties'.

All of these episodes were accompanied by elaborate legends, which consisted mainly of empty words, but together they created a sense of the tremendous work that has been done by the investigators, and they were kind of proving something, but if you look at each of them separately, you can't find anything except verbiage in any of them.

Secondly, it is possible to vilify and demonize the personality of the accused in the eyes of judges and the public, which is particularly important if it is a public trial. In this direction, too, the investigation has worked well.

My simultaneous training at the Academy and possession of the arms business were emphasized. Naturally, the motives for entering the Academy were clearly interpreted as a way to further lobby the interests of the Lavroff Weapons Company. I was also reminded of the combat drill when I ostensibly cowardly threw the population of an entire planet to the enemy, though what cowardice could there be in a combat drill?

They even wrote something about my diplomas and referred to circumstantial evidence of bribery of examiners, but indicated that the investigation had been suspended because the statute of limitations had expired. I knew who to thank for that part of the indictment, but it didn't make me feel any better.

And finally, witnesses. It's a separate and very bright song. If you want it badly, the investigator can almost always find the key to a middle-level official. An official caught in bribery or embezzlement and knowing that there is no escape from punishment is willing to cooperate with investigation to avoid a real prison term. Among other things, such official is ready to work as a 'speaking head' in those criminal trials that the investigator indicates.

Now, there are three minor officials of the Ministry of Defence I've actually met once or twice, And who, as it turned out, were sitting on the EFSS's hook. These gentlemen, looking me in the eye at the confrontations, assured the investigator with genuine sincerity that I had offered them bribes, but they bravely refused.

As a cherry on top, I was charged with embezzling part of the advance from the Ministry of Defence on the contract. The Lavroff Weapons Company did indeed spend part of this money on equipment not used directly for the work under the contract with the Ministry of Defence, but it did not affect the timing and quality of the work. The investigator listened to my explanation absent-mindedly, and it was obvious that for him this was just another episode intended to finally sink the defendant in court.

After reading the case file, my lawyer breathed a heavy sigh, "This is a difficult case. It's obvious to me that the case is fabricated, but this avalanche of negativity could be a bad influence on the judges and the jury. In addition, there is now such a wave on the net. The Russian Weapons Concern is being spread in splinters. There were indeed some bad facts that were skilfully inflated up to the treason of the Motherland. And in this story, the Lavroff Arms Company is constantly implicated. It's all in words, but public opinion, you know, it's a controlled thing. Well, I'll do whatever it takes to break most of the charges, maybe all of them, if the judges aren't completely biased, but we need a backup trump card, 'cause I can't guarantee that we'll fight back just by law."

"And what trump card is that?"

"Your Gold Star and Iron Cross. There's a war going on right now, and you have the highest combat awards, which makes a difference. There are certain privileges in the statutes of these orders for their knights. Not many people know such details, in wartime, in case of criminal prosecution of the holder of any of these orders, it is possible to discontinue the case by the way of bringing in the guaranty by the Federation Army high-ranking officers. This possibility does not apply to all articles of the Penal Code, but our case is appropriate. This addition to the statutes of the orders was made at the beginning of the war, during the most difficult years, when every good soldier and officer could swing the scales one way or the other."

"Ten high-ranking officers? What do the guarantors risk?"

"If, however, the allegations are substantiated, their careers might be adversely affected. But to do that, the evidence has to be really hard."

"To be honest, Sergei," I told the lawyer with doubt, "I don't know if there are so many generals and admirals willing to risk their careers for me. And you just told me about the negative wave."

"As a last resort, I'll alert any potential guarantors you've served or crossed paths with. It will be a public trial, they will be able to see and decide for themselves."

"All right, Sergei, let's do this," I agreed and after some contemplation I continued, "Since the situation has taken such a tough turn, I think it's time to put all the cards on the table. Contact Major André Mbia of the 105th Infantry Division. He will give you the evidence of the betrayal that took place during our last operation in the Gliese-338 system. I think the Internal Security Service of the Ministry of Defence might be very interested in these materials."

***

The trial was supposed to take place in two weeks. The GWI lobbyists strained every nerve, and the investigators were in a hurry. The Public Prosecutor's Office was also very prompt and confirmed the indictment in record time. The scandal around the Russian Weapons Concern has reached its maximum, and it's organizers didn't want to miss the opportunity to try the persons involved in this high-profile case at the height of people's wrath.

But RWC wasn't going down without a fight either. The Concern had its lobbyists in State bodies, some media outlets under it's control, and it's own well-fed public figures. Global Weapon Industries began to receive painful injections at vulnerable points, it turned out it had a lot of vulnerabilities just like its competitors.

Some cases against the leaders of the Russian Weapons Concern started to fall apart like card houses. Of course, RWC didn't have as many resources as the GWI, but to break is easier than to build. Breaking up a criminal case is usually easier than bringing it to a logical conclusion.

Philistines went from from one extreme to another, not knowing what was really going on, and why the world went mad overnight, and bulky information manure tanks accumulated over the years by weapons corporations, which quietly stank before then, creating familiar background of minor scandals and minor investigations, these tanks suddenly burst into the net with powerful geysers, pouring everything around with their contents.

My case against this background seemed like a rather minor episode, and yet it managed to attract the attention of many people, including those who knew me personally. When the streams of mud that were flooding my name online have reached their climax, in commentaries on numerous puff pieces and similar puff topics in forums suddenly appeared messages, which apparently didn't not meet the expectations of the customers of these materials.

'It's all crap. And your paper is crap. I fought with Lavroff on Kapteen. If it weren't for him, I'd be rotting in quarg captivity right now or dying of my wounds. And if this man has taken up arms production, I'm calm for our army. Get away from Lavroff, you assholes. Private First Class Anton Gnezdoff. Planetary Commando Special Forces.'

'Who are you accusing of cowardice, half-wits? The cadet who took command of the regiment when all the officers died? The man who recaptured one hundred and fifty of our POW from the quargs on Leiten-5? I owe him my life, and I'm not the only one. He bribed someone? What are you driveling about? I'd believe he punched someone in the face for trying to extort that bribe. What you write is a dirty puff piece. Captain Ivan Ivlev. 105th Infantry Division.'

'Lavroff bought a higher education diploma? I took his biochemistry exam myself. You haven't even bothered to contact me, gentlemen of the press. You can't even lie. Igor Lavroff has saved mankind from asteroid fever. His name is the first name on the patent for the treatment of this recently fatal disease. At the moment, more than a million of our fellow citizens owe their lives to this young man. He bought this, too? Professor Lutsko. The Colonial Technological Institute. Titan.'

'You've lost your bearings, gentlemen. Or rather, just sold yourself. I saw Lavroff in combat when he was still a cadet. My son, also a cadet, came back alive from Leiten-5 because of him. The Heavy Commando Brigade commanded by Lavroff had a combat effectiveness of 132%. You want to deprive our army of such an officer? Open the Criminal Code, gentlemen. There's an article about treason. Familiarize yourself, it might come in handy. Admiral James Fulton. Fifth Strike Fleet.'

'Unfortunately, I don't know Mr Lavroff personally, but in front of my eyes, he fought at the head of two platoons of his men against a full infantry battalion of quargs reinforced with two heavy robots. Lavroff's men fought on machines developed by his company. My life really depended on the results of this fight, and since I'm alive and writing these lines, I can state with certainty: if in order for such machines to enter our army one has to pay bribes, it means that in the Earth Federation something has rotted thru, and we're all about to end. Associate Professor, Indonesian Military Technical University, Major Vening Vulandari. '

Many hundreds of such messages were received unexpectedly quickly. The lawyer read them to me and said that this unexpected support could have a significant impact on the outcome of the case, but apparently, he underestimated the adversary.

Corruption cases have been tried by Earth Federation courts only in open court and in jury trials only. The open regime meant not only being able to come to court in person, but also being present virtually, online.

To my surprise, a very large courtroom was full. Used to getting all the necessary information online, people nevertheless decided to spend their time and come to court in person. The court officials were not accustomed to such pandemonium and evidently felt nervous.

I was taken to a small room, separated from the courtroom by transparent walls, where I was left alone. The only way I could communicate with the court and the jury was by means of acoustic system built into the surface of the table.

When the composition of the court and the jury were presented before the hearing, my lawyer only shook his head.

"Igor, I haven't seen such lawlessness in a long time. The president of the court appears to be relatively independent, but has a reputation of a very murky type. One of the judges is just a GWI man, the other one also probably is, although I'm not 100% sure. Six out of eight jurors are henchmen of our opponents. One of the others is RWC man, and I'm not sure why they sent him here. I can't say anything about the last juror, but it doesn't change anything. It will be the the guilty verdict for sure, but we will still fight. The more ridiculous the sentence, the more likely it is to be appealed."

"What about the guarantors?"

"It's the last resort. I don't want to bet everything on it. You're not sure of it yourself, but if anything, we'll have to try, otherwise, they'll eat you up. "

The trial proved to be a shortened version of the investigation. The same witnesses who said the same words were invited. The results of the investigations were read out, the recordings of my meetings with the officials were shown and the legends fabricated by the investigators were revealed. However, all these exercises were interrupted by my lawyer's speeches, who was slowing down this negative information barrage and beat one argument after another out of the prosecutor's hands.

At one point, I thought the case was starting to unravel. The prosecution's statements were followed by a growl in the courtroom, but the judges turned out to be hardened bureaucratic fighters, and they didn't even have an ear for it.

The way the judges and the prosecutor talked to my lawyer was like a deaf person talking to a blind person. It also started to annoy the public in the courtroom, and the noise increased. The judge called for order and silence, and due to the threat of removal from the courtroom, the noise has decreased.

The case was nearing a verdict. Finally, the judge gave the defense the floor for the final performance. My lawyer based his speech on the most vivid of the messages from the net he read to me before, with his comments and references to sources of information. The people in the courtroom were very impressed with his speech, at least the applause didn't go away for long. The judges and jurors remained imperturbable.

Court adjourned for jury decision, and the jury went into the conference room. We didn't have to wait long. Half an hour later, the trial resumed with a verdict.

"By seven votes in favour, with one against the jury, citizen Lavroff Igor Yakovlevich was found guilty of all counts in the indictment."

The audience muttered. There were even a few loud shouts, but the president of the court again called the meeting to order and was about to announce the removal of the court for a sentencing hearing, when my lawyer raised his hand to get his attention.

"Your Honor," - Sergei Isaev spoke loud and clear, "The defense insists on a special procedure in the case of citizen Lavroff, based on the statutes of the Gold Star and the Iron Cross, of which he is the Knight."

The judge lost his temper for a second. Either he hoped it wouldn't come to this, or he didn't want to delay sentencing, but his face flinched, however, he quickly regained control of it. He could not refuse. That would be such a gross violation of procedure, that this alone would be a sufficient ground for appeal and subsequent annulment of the sentence.

"The Court granted the defence motion," the President responded with an ice-cold voice, "In accordance with the statute of the above-mentioned Orders, the high-ranking officers of the Army of the Earth Federation may provide guarantees for the defendant. If such guarantors are ten or more, the criminal prosecution of the defendant will be suspended until the end of the hostilities, and all charges will be dropped. The statutes of the orders and other laws and regulations do not specify the exact time within which at least 10 guarantees must be provided. It is simply stated that this should be done within a reasonable time. Thus, the time during which the court will accept guarantees is left to the discretion of the court itself. Bearing in mind the public nature of the trial, as well as the webcasting of the proceedings and the possibility of providing guarantee remotely, the court determines that the guarantees for citizen Lavroff must be submitted within thirty minutes from the moment of the announcement of the decision, starting now."

It was a pity to look at Sergei. My lawyer clearly did not expect such a blow below the belt. And he could not object to the court, it was true that the law did not set specific time limits for providing of guarantees, and there was no established court practice on the subject, this provision of the law was too rarely invoked in the courts.

The people in the courtroom were once again indignantly buzzing and were no longer responding to the president's calls for silence and order.

The sudden melodic signal silenced the hall. The signal came from the working place of the clerk of Court.

"A guarantee has been provided for the citizen Lavroff," the secretary announced, "Admiral Fulton, Fifth Strike Fleet, vouches that the charges against citizen Lavroff are false and that the loss of this officer by the Earth Federation army could have a significant impact on the timing and the possibility of winning the war."

The courtroom went noisy again, this time with excitement and approval.

The melodic signal sounded again.

"A guarantee has been provided for the citizen Lavroff. Lieutenant General Shiller, director of the Planetary Commando Academy vouches..."

The signal repeated.

"... Commander of the Seventh Commando Corps Colonel General Knyazeff vouches..."

"... Commander of the Fifth Strike Fleet Admiral Nelson vouches..."

"...Chairman of the Council of the Planetary Commando Academy's board of trustees, General of the Army Vasnetsov vouches..."

The courtroom roared. No one was listening to the chairman, and the court guard didn't even try to do anything, making sure the agitated crowd doesn't leave the visitor area.

"...professor of the General Staff Academy Colonel General Swirsky vouches..."

It's been almost 20 minutes. The President of the Court looked with a straight face at the clock, and with each passing minute, his face was softened and he was radiating more confidence.

"...The Chairman of the New Equipment and Weapons Commission of the Ministry of Defense, General of the Army Barrington vouches..."

"Lieutenant General Alatas, Director of the Indonesian Military Technical University, vouches..."

The President of the Court has once again become hysterical. There were five minutes left, and eight guarantees had already been provided.

Only I realised that the list of generals and admirals I had anything to do with the service was almost exhausted, and the judge worries in vain. There's no one else to vouch for me. Two minutes passed in a tense silence. All the more louder and more unexpected was the signal of the incoming official appeal to the court, which was so eagerly awaited by the courtroom.

"...The Chief of the General Staff Academy, General of the Army O'Sullivan vouches..."

I never expected a guarantee from the head of the Academy, but I found it more enjoyable to get one. But there was no more than two minutes left, and there was no last guarantee. Everybody was waiting in silence.

The signal came in at the end of the 29th minute. The Chairman flinched in his place. The clerk looked at the message, but instead of announcing it, he went into some strange state, he read and reread it again and again in complete confusion.

"Secretary, read incoming message," the President of the Court couldn't handle it and roared spitefully on his assistant.

The clerk of Court woke up from the numbness and said in a wooden voice:

"A guarantee has been provided for the citizen Lavroff. Supreme Commander-in-Chief of the Armed Forces of the Earth Federation, Marshal Tobolsky vouches..."

Chapter 6

I was released from custody in a courtroom, and from that point on, the whole thing was reversed. Before I could get to my room at the Academy, my communicator was called by a hidden caller.

"Mr Lavroff," the man's voice politely addressed me, "This is Senior Lieutenant Karjalainen speaking, Ministry of Defense Internal Security. Do you have a few minutes?"

"I'm listening to you."

"Congratulations on dropping all charges, Mr Lavroff. They looked ridiculous, and I hope that you and your company will never again experience such abuse of rights."

"Thank you, Senior Lieutenant. I, too, welcome the outcome of this case, but I think you didn't just call to congratulate me."

"Of course, not only for this," Karjalainen agreed, "I would like to invite you to join us in order to discuss the actions of a group of unidentified persons, which led to the distortion of intelligence about enemy forces in the area of the scientific laboratory in the Glise-338 system. I understand that you've just been released, so I'm not asking for an immediate meeting, but..."

"Senior Lieutenant," I mildly interrupted Karjalainen - "In such cases, wasting time often has extremely painful consequences. Where should I come?"

***

Literally in a day or two, the frenzy of the online media assault on the Russian Weapons Concern has sharply weakened, and the attacks on the Lavroff Arms Company were grinding to a halt. Not only that, denials and even apologies with vague excuses for the mistakes of journalists who did not scrutinize the information with due diligence appeared on the front pages of many media that have covered our name in..., well, call it mud, in recent weeks.

The reason for this was the violent activity of Sergei Isaev. Well inspired by the outcome of the case he didn't exactly hope to win, my lawyer started filing libel suits against the online publications that stigmatized us the most, and these suits were just flying off his desk. The media got hurt. Hot fires flared under their owners' asses, and gentlemen of the press didn't want to take the cases to court.

Arrested RWC functionaries suddenly turned out to be not so nasty bribe takers and embezzlers of public funds, as it seemed a few days ago, they were insensibly released from detention on their own recognizance with a perspective to escape with a fine, or a short suspended sentence. And the lobbyists of Global Weapon Industries, who have expressed themselves best, suddenly found themselves in pre-trial detention and being interrogated by the Ministry of Defence's internal security investigators.

I applauded President Tobolsky in my mind, although I can't say I've been very happy with my role in this whole story, it's not nice to be a pawn in someone else's game, and the President used me in that capacity. I understand Tobolsky wanted to provoke the GWI into action. He needed a serious irritant, which GWI management would like to eliminate, and to do that they would have to open up and use its administrative resources and cross relatively safe boundaries.

He did it brilliantly. He threw into an entrenched swamp with full and satisfied frogs the arrogant and determined Second Lieutenant who, by his actions, raised a wave that shook the plump inhabitants and forced them to act recklessly. As you can see, the GWI thought it was a good situation to get rid of the unexpected, very active, but still a small competitor, and at the same time bite off a fair piece of the market controlled by the Russian Weapons Concern. But the snatched piece got stuck in its throat, and then the blow came out of nowhere, and everything the GWI blamed the Lavroff Weapons Company and RWC for, suddenly was hurled on the lobbyists and functionaries of Global Weapon Industries by the Ministry of Defence Internal Security.

The President, on the other hand, has shown no sign of himself until the very last moment, but in the end, when the absurdity of what happened began to reach even ordinary people, he intervened very effectively providing me a guarantee in the high-profile lawsuit. On the one hand, he did not formally put any direct pressure on the court, and, on the other hand, demonstrated to everybody that he would not tolerate lawlessness and ensure order in the Federation. That's the combination that makes a pawn in the person of Mr Lavroff successfully reach the opposite end of the chessboard and turn into... not a queen, of course, it would be too much for such a pawn. Rather, it turned into a light figure, a bishop or a knight, which is not bad for a pawn.

Thanks for not swapping for an enemy pawn. Although, in this case, I've been floundering myself most of the time. The President just helped me stir up a swamp by recommending my company's license, and then the pawn moved on its own, and if it was eaten on the way, the grandmaster-president would shrug his shoulders and forget it existed. But when the pawn was about to do its work, he remembered it, and didn't let the enemy whisk it off the board by a careless movement. Thanks for that, too. We'll still make it to the queen. And let's not forget, in these backroom chess games, the pieces on the board can sometimes turn into players, although it's quite rare.

***

We were fulfilling the order quite on schedule. After the joint repulse of the GWI attack, our relationship with the Russian Weapons Concern has only improved, and RWC worked harder than ever to get us the components we need without delay or disruption.

All of a sudden, I got an invitation to a meeting from General Barrington. Apparently, under the contract with the Ministry of Defense, there was no claim against me. Out of a thousand commando platoon packs, we've shipped them more than half. As far as I knew, some of this equipment had already gone to re-equip the commando units, and they haven't filed a complaint yet. But since the General has something to say to me, I'd be happy to talk to him, especially since I wanted to thank him for his guarantee.

General of the Army Barrington met me with a moderate smile.

"Congratulations on your release, Mr Lavroff," he said, extending his hand to me for a handshake.

"Thank you, General of the Army, Sir," I also smiled, "If it weren't for your guarantee, I wouldn't be having the pleasure of talking to you right now."

"You should thank your new developments, Mr Lavroff. I was aware that without your involvement our army would lose them, which would be wrong. And imprisoning a good officer during a war... You know what I mean. By the way, it's your new devices that I wanted to talk to you about when inviting you here."

"Is there something wrong with them?"

"On the contrary, Mr Lavroff. A week ago, the quargs launched an attack on one of the planets of the Grumbridge-1618 system. Apparently, they were planning some kind of reconnaissance in forces, targeting a peripheral, sparsely populated, and loosely terraformed planet, and their forces were small. There was no orbital defence as such, which is why the squadron of quargs, which appeared at the system's borders unexpectedly for our fleet, once again, could have easily made it to the planet and landed commandos.

Our troops were not stationed at Grumbridge-9. All the leadership on the planet had was a police force, who, of course, could not seriously resist commmandos. Ships and troops from the central regions of the system had to be moved urgently to the planet under attack. The Sixth Fleet responded to the threat very quickly, because after Gliese, the combat readiness was maintained. The quargs were ejected from low orbits and then forced to jump and leave the system. They didn't have time to evacuate their landing party, and Colonel General Ivashkevich had to disembark the 65th Commando Division at Grumbridge-9.

One of its regiments received your dropships, robots, and space suits a week before this battle. The quargs were purged surprisingly quickly, with losses of fifty-five percent of the estimated, and at the end of the operation, the Colonel General reported to Navy Admiral Kawakami requesting to expedite as much as possible the re-equipment of his commando corps with these new devices, because its presence fundamentally alters the balance of power in combat in favor of the Federation commandos. Kawakami familiarized himself with the records of the battle and forwarded the application to us with his resolution 'I ask for full cooperation'. We have received similar reviews from other units that have received your devices.

Therefore, I have a question for you, Mr Lavroff, whether your company's production capacity allows you to increase the output of your EW systems and accelerate the modernization of the equipment supplied to you by the Ministry?"

So I started thinking. We can, of course, deploy new production facilities. We're perfectly capable of hiring additional staff, but turning the Lavroff Weapons Company into an industrial giant, that will produce military equipment in thousands of pieces, I didn't plan this at all. I was interested in the creation and introduction of new technologies, the development of breakthrough weapons, and not the production of huge batches of machines that have already been tested in battle. Let others who have both the production facilities and the experience of large-scale production do it.

"General of the Army, Sir," I responded after a small pause, "We could do that, but we don't plan to produce large quantities of military products. We are ready to transfer the technology and all our know-how related to these devices to any major company capable of producing them in series. It won't be free, of course, because the

Lavroff Weapons Company needs funds for basic research and for the development of new samples of weapons and equipment."

"This is a very reasonable proposition for the benefit of the Federation, Mr Lavroff, but it's very unexpected to hear that from the head of a private company. Do you realize what potential profits you're losing here?"

"Of course. But I expect to compensate for all these losses with future revenues from our new developments. We already have prototypes that suggest that. In addition, our company will still be the main contractor for the new larger contract, and we'll sub-contract the rest."

"Apply for the competition, Mr Lavroff. The Ministry of Defence is ready to order from the Lavroff Weapons Company the new EW complexes for 15,000 dropships, Goannas and sets of space suits. In fact, this is the rearmament of all landing units in our army."

"Thank you for your trust, General of the Army, Sir."

"Don't let me down, Mr Lavroff. I have earned my reputation by supplying troops with all the necessities during the most difficult years of the war. Now these hard years are returning, and I want to restore to our Army the reliable rear and the uninterrupted supply of the best equipment the Federation can produce. And I'm counting on you for that."

***

I was holding the thin plate of the new processor, and I was remembering the anguish we had to endure with it. My knowledge, of course, has been very helpful, but the technology difference between the worlds of Brigadier General Dean and Lieutenant Igor Lavroff remained very large. We had to do all kinds of tricks and replace parts that are publicly available in my world with bewitching articles using local technology. As a result, the size of the processor was ten times that of the original, but it didn't really scare me. A combat robot is a big thing, there should be plenty of room.

I was wondering where to start. The processor I was holding gave me a wide margin for choice. Its main purpose is to control the external sensors and all filling of combat scanners, communication devices and EW complexes. For the most efficient use of those software algorithms, which have made it possible in my world to overcome the decades-long predominance of radio-electronic warfare means over means of communication, such a specially designed processor architecture was required. And now the key component of the circuitry was slightly cooling my fingers. We've done it.

I am a commando. I've been one my whole life in that world, and I've become a commando in this world. I've got my whole being attached to this branch of troops, and in another role I could hardly imagine myself, but at the same time, I realized that commandos, and in general, ground troops alone could not win the modern space war.

The Earth Federation needed a strong fleet and it wasn't there. No matter how much I improve the ground forces' weapons, I can't turn the tide of the war, it became very clear to me. Well, we commandos, have something to offer the Fleet, too. It may seem exotic to many, but it's worth a try.

I've assembled my entire science and engineering department, headed by Professor Stein and Chief Engineer Jeff.

"Gentlemen," I told my staff, "you've done a great job. You have made a device that will allow our company to take a leading position in the market. In time, of course, but that time will come soon enough, no doubt. But the most important thing, this plate here" - I showed the staff the processor that's still being squeezed in my hand - "will make it possible to accelerate our victory. On this occasion, I will award everyone a bonus equivalent to annual salary to everyone of you. You have earned this."

The approval noise was the answer, but these guys knew me well and were waiting for a follow-up. Naturally, it ensued.

"Now, colleagues, I would like to present your department with a rather untrivial task. We'll be making remote-controlled assault drones. The point is, there is one manned combat robot, the pilot of which controls a dozen drones under his command. It used to be impossible because of unreliable communications, which would have led to a permanent breakdown in control, but now we have this," I demonstrated the processor to the assembled people again, "which means we have uninterrupted communication between the pilot and the satellite machines. The challenge is that unmanned machines must be highly autonomous. Pilot of the control module, let's call it a command machine, can't control every gun and every drone movement, as a pilot of a conventional combat robot does. Accordingly, we need a powerful computer in every drone, and, above all, a reliable software algorithm that will allow the drone to operate in battle. I'll take care of this part of the design. The rest is up to you. I want to see the basic concept by tomorrow night.

As guinea pigs, I'm thinking of using a dozen trophy Mammoths captured on Leiten-5. I'm sure the Ministry of Defense will not refuse to hand over these robots to the Lavroff Weapons Company for experimental purposes."

***

"Lieutenant Lavroff?" the Colonel General Knyazev was a little surprised, as I used the direct contact he gave me after the battle of Leiten-5, for the first time, "I'm glad to see you, officer. What happened to you?"

"Nothing as bad as a 15-year sentence, Colonel General, Sir," I smiled, "By the way, thank you for your guarantee."

"Assholes," the General answered briefly.

"I totally agree with you, Colonel Gen..."

"Put the ranks aside, Lieutenant."

"Yes, Sir. Well, Pavel Grigoryevich, I need your advice. Not as a lieutenant, but as the head of the Lavroff Weapons Company. I'd like to show you our latest development. I'm not asking for your help in promoting it in the Ministry of Defence, but I need your opinion on the prospect of a new approach that we have adopted."

"A general is always interested in seeing a new weapon," grinned Knyazev, "Where and when?"

"It would be ideal, of course, to hold a demonstration at the Planetary Commando Academy range on Ganymede, but I understand that leaving troops for such a flight..."

"I won't have to leave anyone behind. We're going with the Fifth Strike Fleet to the Solar System for reinforcement and partial rearmament. I've seen your developments, by the way, although not in a battle yet. That's impressive. When can we expect a complete re-equipment of commando units?"

"The Ministry of Defence has already signed a new contract with us. I think it's gonna take at least six months."

"That's too long, Lieutenant, too long! I feel like everything's gonna start turning a lot sooner. Okay, when do you want to see me?"

"We'll be ready in a couple of weeks. Except, Pavel Grigorievich, I have one more request. Could you invite Admiral Nelson to my demonstration?"

"What for? He's never been interested in our land affairs."

"I have something to offer the Fleet, but I need the Admiral's support. Again, it's nothing to do with lobbying, I'm just gonna need to run and test our novelties somewhere, in conditions close to combat. This will require ships, and my company does not yet have a war fleet of its own."

"Yet?" The General raised his eyebrow ironically.

"Who knows how it's gonna turn around? I wouldn't mind."

***

Lieutenant General Shiller, as Director of the Academy and, accordingly, master of the Ganymede Range, received the guests in his office. Knyazev and Nelson seemed interested, and Shiller, who had already seen our products, fueled their interest with slight hints and sort of casual reservations. Eventually, they decided not to delay the case, and together they went to the range far out of town.

I was already there with my team. At first, I thought I'd climb into the command robot's cockpit and personally demonstrate to the Generals and Admiral a new concept of battle, but Inga spent the night convincing me in every way she could that she could do it as well as I could, and I'll be much more useful in the bunker next to the high-ranking guests. Well, I can't say which arguments have affected me more, but I finally agreed to it in the morning.

"Gentlemen," I started the presentation of our new products, "You're looking at some of the heavy quarg Mammoth robots you know. But this is only by appearance. In fact, nine of them have no cockpit at all, they're fully automated, the pilot's former location is now occupied by additional computers and an increased ammunition stockpile. Only the command car remained manned."

"Khm..." hemmed Knyazev with doubt, "and how will all this be managed in battle?"

"Now, Cadet Kotova will show you this," I promised, "We'll conduct a battle drill of a dozen of our Mammoths with a cadet commando company. Naturally, the balance of power is clearly in favor of the Mammoths, but I want to show you not so much their firepower, which you yourself are well aware of, but rather the driveability and the behaviour of unmanned vehicles in combat with the intensive use of electronic countermeasures by the enemy."

"Well, let's see," the Admiral said. The look on Nelson's face showed him to be curious, but he had no real interest. That's okay, we'll get to your flying pieces of iron, Admiral, bear with it a little.

General Shiller gave the order, and the combat machines at the range started to move. Inga didn't trick me. That was for good reason, when, with Shiller's permission, she was busting her hump running the Mammoths on the range, now everything worked out just beautiful. The Mammoths held the battle formation perfectly, bombarded the poor Goannas with rockets and cannon shells, shot down the rockets flying to them in response, and, in general, showed themselves being irrepressible in battle.

"What means of EW are being used?" - asked me Knyazev, "I don't see any impact of their work. Your Mammoths are maneuvering as if no one was trying to disrupt their connection to the commander's machine."

"Commando company standard EW complexes were first operational. In the second minute, stationary battalion EW stations were added to them. Another minute later, we added the latest developments of the Russian Weapons Concern, and now our latest EW complexes, with which the dropships recently brought into service in your corps are equipped, are also working."

"Don't talk nonsense, Lieutenant Lavroff," Admiral Nelson resented it, "It doesn't just happen."

"But that's just it, Admiral."

"Umm…, well, then, let's do this," pronounced Nelson, taking out his communicator, "Moscow cruiser, enter a low orbit above the Planetary Commando Academy range. Use the EW means to jam communications all over the range."

In the meantime, the battle drill ended, as expected, with a total victory for the Mammoths. However, their opponent was not equal.

Looking at the Admiral, Knyazev grinned:

"Lieutenant General, Sir," he told Shiller, "Do you mind if we do a little landing drill here? I'm interested in seeing how these unmanned robots play out against our manned Bisons with experienced pilots."

"Yes, please, gentlemen. That's why you came here," Shiller calmly answered.

"Transport Pretoria to land a division of heavy robots at the Planetary Commando Academy training ground. In training equipment, of course," commanded Knyazev via the communicator and, having listened back, continued, "Yes, with an escort, as in combat. And add them the reinforced divisional level EW complex."

The director of the academy's communicator issued a silent signal. The General responded to the call.

"Lieutenant General, Sir, this is the Ganymede Civil Administration Secretariat. We're seeing increased activity of warships in the vicinity of the colony's capital. We weren't warned about this. You got this under control?"

"Don't worry, it's just a small joint drill between the Planetary Commando Academy and the Fifth Strike Fleet. Everything is under control, nothing threatens the infrastructure and the dwellers of the capital."

"You've never done this before, Lieutenant General, Sir, but we understand. Thank you," and the caller hung up.

"The civilians are wondering what kind of fuss we made in low orbits," Shiller smiled, "I calmed them down."

In the meantime, the cruiser entered a low orbit and activated electronic jamming systems.

"Cadet Kotova," I told Inga via my personal communicator, "Demonstrate to the High Commission the efficiency of your unmanned personnel."

Inga had a peculiar sense of humor, which I was very impressed with. Now, she's found nothing better than to fire five rockets from the unmanned Mammoths backpack launchers in the belly of a cruiser, hovering in low orbit, and by doing so, she showed that the connection to the drones was working very well. The missiles were training, of course, but the cruiser's captain was offended and tried to cover up insolent ground cockroaches with controlled bombs. Those bombs were also training, of course. Such munitions did not contain lethal elements or powerful explosive charges, but they produced plausible light-noise effects imitating a detonation. In near-space and on the surface, flashes and explosions sparked.

Shiller's communicator gave a signal again.

"Lieutenant General, Sir," a nervous voice was heard from the device, "this is the outer orbital post Callisto 14. We're watching a battle in orbit around Ganymede. What's going on?"

"Ehh..., gentlemen, don't worry. This is a drill. We're working with the Fifth Strike Fleet to practice combat team-work of the fleet and the landing forces. We have everything under control."

"I've got you. Thank you for your information, Lieutenant General, Sir."

In the meantime, a full Bison division with reinforcements has landed on the surface. This isn't a cadet company. The fight was serious.

Inga's Mammoths stubbornly resisted attempts to disrupt their communications with the command machine, and Inga herself, with great enthusiasm, fired guided missiles at Bisons, and these missiles somehow got off course far less often than heavy robot pilots were used to.

Admiral Nelson, frustrated by the failure of the Moscow cruiser, decided to add pepper to the brew:

"Aircraft-carrier Windhoek to raise the pursuit planes and attack the training targets at the Planetary Commando Academy range, simulating atmospheric attack planes."

At the Planetary Commando Academy range, relatively small and utterly unprepared for such a large-scale exercise, an epic battle was waged using all branches of the armed forces. Tons of training ammunition burned, engines of the cosmic pursuit planes, completely unsuitable for atmospheric flights, roared wildly, heavy robots heatedly exchanged missile salvos, and electronic warfare has reached such a level that the civilian communications networks of the capital of Ganymede have become intermittent.

The militant General and an equally militant Admiral saw before them a weapon that could change the course of a war, and they were anxious to fully test it.

Shiller's communicator rang for the third time.

"Lieutenant General Shiller, what's going on over there? This is General of the Army Vasnetsov. What? I hardly hear you, Drill? What the fuck is your drill? Why don't I know? Do you know what it looks like from Earth? So, you don't know? Well, I'll tell you. It looks like storming Ganymede! I'm sick of panicking screams. They almost sent the Metropolitan fleet to you. What? New weapon? This Lavroff guy again? We shouldn't provide him guarantees, we'd be more comfortable. So, in short, Lieutenant General, stop the fireworks and wait for me and General of the Army Barrington. We're also interested in seeing what kind of toy your Lavroff gave into the playful hands of Nelson and Knyazev, so that they made half of the Solar system panicking."

Generals of the Army Barrington and Vasnetsov arrived at Ganymede three hours later. As ordered, the drills were suspended, but the Bisons and the Mammoths were still in departure positions, and the ships of the Fifth Strike Fleet came closer to Ganymede, awaiting orders from their Admiral.

And so it all started anew, but the more discreet, apparently by virtue of their age, Generals of the Army did find the strength to stop in time the militaristic bacchanal.

"Well, gentlemen, it's enough for today," summarized the demonstration General Barrington, "we'll continue tomorrow, but not here. Stop scaring the civilian population of Ganymede. Mr Lavroff, do you have a chance to relocate your robots to Callisto by tomorrow?"

"There's an entire Strike Fleet above us, General of the Army," Admiral Nelson answered for me, "What is a dozen heavy robots to us?"

"Accepted. And here's the thing, Mr Lavroff. Tomorrow, I'm coming to Callisto as part of the New Equipment and Weapons Commission of the Ministry of Defense. I understand that you weren't preparing for a state acceptance of your specimens, but what I saw... Well, we can't afford to stall when our army needs machines like this. And one more thing. What prompted you to create a drone unit? This is a completely new word in our military doctrine, and also in the quarg doctrine."

"General of the Army, Sir, I believe that a soldier in the armored space suit has no place on the modern battlefield. It's a relic holding on to which we take a heavy toll in people. How long and how much money does it take to train one good infantryman? What's his combat effectiveness compared to a combat robot? We have to keep our people safe, and we send them into battle sometimes in light armor. A saboteur or a scout is another matter. The armored space suits fit them as best they can, but the line infantry must disappear from the army. It will be replaced by unmanned drones. It's now that we've set up a semi-division of heavy robots as an example, but we're already working on lighter models to replace a squad of commandos. There's gonna be one live pilot in a dropship, in the command machine. The rest are his commanded assault drones. This will increase the survivability of an individual combat unit, losses in people will be reduced by a factor, and one of the main characteristics of a unit - density of fire - will reach a new level."

Barrington looked at me, wanted to ask me something else, but all he ended up saying was, "I've heard you, Mr

Lavroff. At fourteen tomorrow, be ready to receive my Commission."

Chapter 7

On Callisto, we had no problem.

The Commission no longer included lobbyists from Global Weapon Industries, and Barrington's new aides, Lieutenant General and Vice Admiral, were quite the sane people, who were very interested in the new concept.

After the trials ended, Nelson and Knyazev pulled me aside.

"Lieutenant," told me Nelson, who consistently treated me like an officer, not the head of a private company, "Colonel General Knyazev called me here to show your novelty. Well, I'll be honest, I was very interested, although your development has nothing to do with my specialty. But I was promised you could surprise me with something useful to the Fleet. Is that right?"

"That's right, Admiral, Sir."

"I'm listening to you very carefully."

"Admiral, Sir, I have two concepts for you. So far, these are just ideas, but their realization for ground forces you've just seen. The first, imagine ten cosmic pursuit planes, only one of which is piloted by a human. This is the exact equivalent of what you saw yesterday and today at the range."

"The idea is clear," Nelson nodded, "and the other?"

"Now, imagine this: there's a squadron fight going on. How often do pursuit planes manage to break through close to enemy heavy ships?"

"It happens in every battle, but what can a pursuit plane do with it's weapon to a battleship? Here we need large-caliber guns or torpedoes. Pursuit planes don't carry them."

"But a dozen drones the size of a pursuit plane are quite capable of dropping several dozen assault drones on board an enemy ship."

"Boarding in space?!" The Admiral was truly surprised, "We never try to capture even the heavily damaged enemy ships. There's too much chance of self-destructing of a ship under threat of capture. No one's prepared to risk people like that."

"I don't talk of people, Admiral, Sir. I suggest we send a group of drones controlled from outside to board. When they enter the enemy ship, they begin to destroy the crew and the most important sets and units. The ship can no longer fight at full strength, and it's coming out of the fight," I didn't tell Nelson about another opportunity that hadn't been fully worked out. I wanted to apply my experience of intercepting the control of enemy equipment, which was very useful to me at Leiten-5 and Kapteen, but for enemy ships.

"And how will your drones be controlled once they've boarded the ship? The signal from the outside won't get in, and the return signal won't come out."

"We thought of it. The problem is solved by a chain of transponders. I won't bore you with the details, but technically it's possible."

"You know, Lieutenant, if someone else told me this, I wouldn't listen to him, but what I saw today convinces me that you're not just talking air. What exactly do you want from me?"

"Ten of the pursuit planes that are about to be discarded, but still working, and the possibility to conduct battle drills involving your ships, when I have something to test, naturally."

"Prepare your drones, Lieutenant. This is my personal contact. Send me the coordinates for the planes to be delivered. I want machines like those too, he's not the only one," Nelson nodded towards Knyazev, "and it's not three days to prepare a pursuit plane pilot, by the way, and there's always a shortage of pilots in the Fleet."

***

The Callisto test set a precedent unparalleled in the Earth Federation. The Ministry of Defence has placed an order with a private company to develop several types of new weapons. Government institutes and universities were usually involved in this. Private companies, of course, did their research, but only at their own expense, and handed over to the Ministry of Defence prototypes of military equipment at tests. In this case, no ready prototypes were available, because we just upgraded the captured quarg robots. So the Ministry of Defence ordered us to develop drones controlled by a commanding robot's pilot for commandos and infantrymen, and for the fleet, pursuit plane drones that play the role of supporting aircrafts attached to a manned lead plane.

In addition, I convinced Barrington to fund the creation of boarding robots and their carriers. The idea seemed dubious to the General, but I was supported by Admiral Nelson, and the Vice Admiral who was on the committee was interested in this concept.

We now had a rare moment when money, resources and people were available. We worked like slaves on the plantations, but in strange ways we enjoyed it. I used to come crawling to the Academy on my last legs, it took me a while to notice that in such cases instructors didn't bother me, whether by understanding the reasons for my condition, or by having the proper instructions from management. I didn't like it, but I took the situation for granted, trying at least not to fail the test assignments. It almost always worked. Major Linden disappeared from the group without a trace. The second Major went with him and the Captain stayed, but he was quiet, only occasionally throwing cautious but angry looks at me.

We didn't have a new equipment for the first test until two and a half months later, and I immediately knocked on Admiral Nelson's comms.

"Admiral, Sir, I'm ready to report to your fleet's deployment site with my products."

"What do you want to bring, Lieutenant?"

"Nine pilotless pursuit planes and a commander's plane. Plus ten carriers based on the pursuit plane, with five boarding drones each. And for Colonel General Knyazev three squads of assault drones and three commander's machines."

"Good. My fleet is now in the Ross-154 star system. In two days, new aircraft carrier Wellington leaves the Solar System for our deployment site. It should form part of the Fifth Strike Fleet. Captain Clark will take on board your team and all necessary equipment. I will instruct him to accommodate you and allow you to prepare for your trials. You will work from the aircraft carrier, it'll be convenient in every way."

***

On board the aircraft carrier we looked like crows of khaki color against the background of blue navy uniforms, attracting everybody's attention. Our equipment was even more interesting. No one paid much attention to the landing dropships modestly standing in one of the hangars, but around the pilotless pursuit planes and the carriers of boarding drones, the Fleet guys kept walking around in circles, genuinely perplexed at what these Army men are doing here, and with evidently Fleet equipment.

After all, Captain Clark couldn't help but question me in detail about the appointment of our machines. The idea of pilotless pursuit planes caused him to be very skeptical, and during one of the hiatus between the hyperjumps, he offered me a battle drill between my machines and ten of his pursuit planes. I didn't refuse, of course. Any such effort is part of the test, and therefore is only to my advantage. But I was the only one who was able to pilot the commander's plane, and I'm really not much of a pursuit plane pilot. I mean, I've piloted Cuirassier and the dropships, but that's not it at all.

In the end, as expected, my piloting was mediocre at best, but my unmanned subordinates did pretty well. Of course, they acted in a routine manner, using ready-made battle algorithms embedded in their computer brains, but they didn't make mistakes, first of all, and second, they could afford more active maneuvering and higher ammunition consumption. And finally, the latest-model RW stations have been very helpful, too.

We were circling the aircraft carrier, playing one of the typical battle scenarios - encounter battle. I prioritized targets and controlled drone fire, trying not to get caught up in enemy fire. I've almost always been able to do that, but the lack of experience with space warfare, of course, has affected the result, and Captain Clark's experienced pilots finally beat my ten. When I got out of the command plane and reached the carrier's command post, Captain Clark seemed satisfied.

"You were a pretty good fighter, Lieutenant, but you have to admit, 10-5 doesn't support the superiority of your machines."

"I respectfully disagree, Captain, Sir," I allowed myself a little smile, "look carefully at my shoulder straps. You're looking at a lieutenant commando, in other words, I beg your pardon, a land rat. What kind of a pursuit plane pilot am I? That's not what I was taught. Nevertheless, your air force lost five trained pilots during the battle drill, while your hypothetical enemy lost only one pilot who was actually a self-taught amateur. Now imagine if I wasn't the pilot of the command plane, but one of your guys, who was so busy chasing my drones today?"

The captain hemmed and thought. He didn't see our fight from that point of view.

"Well, Lieutenant, you have a point. I'd like to train my people on your new machines. Is it possible?"

"I wanted to ask you that myself, Captain, Sir, because it was for you, for the Fleet, that we designed these machines."

***

We joined the fifth strike fleet a week later. During that time, a dozen aircraft carrier pilots test-flew our new machines, and the results of the combat drills have changed accordingly. Drones with one pilot consistently lost to ten piloted planes, but when the battle was fought by professionals on both sides, the average victory was given to the piloted planes at a loss of seven to nine machines.

When Nelson looked at our drills, he hemmed with satisfaction.

"What's that supposed to mean, Lieutenant? One pilot and nine drones can replace at least seven manned machines? "

"That's right, Admiral, Sir. Combat drill statistics confirm that."

"So we can..." The Admiral was interrupted by a sudden emergency call. Nelson listened to the message, changed his countenance and gave the order in an abrupt voice via communicator:

"The Fleet is on alert. Ready to boost in ten minutes."

"Officers, Sirs," the Admiral turned to us again, "quargs attacked Barnard's star system. Six light years from Earth. The Fourth Fleet is fighting in planetary orbits. I'm going back to the flagship. Get ready to jump."

***

Barnard's star was one of the inner systems of the Earth Federation. The colonization of its planets took place long before the invasion of quargs, and after the war began, people had enough time to reliably strengthen the system. It was the orbital fortresses of the planets Barnard-3 and Barnard-5 that offered very strong resistance to the quargs and inflicted serious damage on enemy forward fleets in the second year of the war.

And now, after an 18-year hiatus, the war is back here again, and this time in a much scarier form. The quargs did not stood still in their development and regularly surprised people with new technologies and weapons, but this time they've outdone themselves.

Captain Clark gave me one of the reserve workbenches at the carrier's command post, and I equipped it with the hardware I've taken with me to control carriers of the boarding drones. When we came out of the last jump three million kilometers from Barnard-7 orbit, some of the operators couldn't contain their surprise.

We were all staring hard at the three-dimensional tactical projection on the main screen, and we didn't believe our eyes.

"The Fourth Fleet is gone," Captain Clark stated the obvious in a colorless voice.

The planets were still holding on, because the Federation Armed Forces had many orbital fortresses around them. Instead of the standard four fortresses in orbit, each of the three terraformed planets had eight fortresses around it, all first class. In addition, several tactical groups of ships of the Tenth and Twelfth fleets have been brought into the system. The Admiralty found it impossible to fully expose their areas of responsibility, but still sent help to the attacked system. However, the situation was not merely threatening, but almost catastrophic.

The quarg fleet initially attacked all three planets at once, but apparently the Fourth Fleet, relying on the orbital fortresses, was able to inflict on it appreciable losses, and the quargs have abandoned this tactic. After regrouping, they concentrated their efforts on Barnard-3, the most densely populated planet in the system. It was in the battle for the planet's high orbits that the remnants of the Fourth Fleet were demolished.

"There are unusually many heavy ships in the enemy fleet," said the senior analyst, "52 streamers. And we don't know the type of the largest."

"Give me a picture," Captain commanded, and the image of the giant battleship occupied about a third of the projection screen. The Earth Federation has never built a ship like this, nor the quargs, at least not before. The ship was at least three times the size of the largest known battleship. The main-calibre weapons placed in the central part of the hull were impressive in their calibre. Right now, the ship was firing, and the barrels of it's cannons lit up with a multi-kilometer red-purple flashes of starting discharges, which rendered the projectiles semi-submerged in hyper. This gave them the ability to move at close to the speed of light. But luckily for both sides, the shells couldn't hit the target at that speed. Physical laws prevented this way of moving near large masses. Having flown a few dozen kilometers from its own ship, the projectiles entered U-mode, and they went out into ordinary space about the same distance from the target.

As a result, a projectile with a typical speed of several kilometres per second reached the enemy's ship.

Aircraft carrier scanners haven't been able to make out the details yet, but we were getting a picture from the ships in the thick of the battle. The Fifth Strike Fleet, struggling with its engines, sought to reach the battlefield. With every new detail added to the tactical projection, it became clearer that it would be extremely difficult to hold the system. The enemy outnumbered us almost three times in quantity of heavy ships, and that's not to mention the giant battleship, which was not even clear as to which class it belonged.

"I mean, it's had it, too," said Captain Clark increasing the portion of the side of the enemy ship on the screen. There were holes in the armoured plates caused by the impact of torpedoes or heavy projectiles.

"This is the result of the counterattack of the Fourth Fleet's line forces," commented the senior analyst, "Unfortunately, Admiral Shimanski lost his last heavy ships in it and died himself with the flagship."

In front of our eyes, one of the orbital fortresses of Barnard-3 flickered and swollen in a glaring burst of internal explosion from the impact of several heavy projectiles which penetrated the armour already weakened by previous damage. The luminous tongues of hot gases and fine particles spewed out from the holes in the armor. The hull split into several pieces, which slowly, by cosmic standards, began to fly in different directions, leaving behind the tails of the fall-off armored metal and the wreckage of the internal structure.

The main forces of the quargs, which were keeping at respectful distance from the planet, turned on the marching engines, and began to move to the resulting weak spot in the defense of the planet. Three battleships and one and a half dozen cruisers from the Tenth and Twelfth fleets regrouped to meet the new threat, but the balance of forces made it obvious they couldn't hold out much longer.

The Fifth Strike Fleet arrived on time, but with its forces, we could hope, just to delay the inevitable. The giant quarg battleship was slowly gaining speed as it approached the planet, and Admiral Nelson had to decide what to do next, although, in fact, he had no choice. Nelson had no right or desire to retreat. All he could do was take as many enemies with him as he could into nonexistence.

"Orbital fortresses, change positions," the Admiral ordered, moving their pictograms on tactical projection to the right points. This maneuver would have closed the gap in defense, but it took the armored 'turtles' more than an hour to complete. "Aircraft carriers Windhoek and Wellington, lift torpedo bombers and provide for them pursuit planes cover. The target is the enemy's flagship. Battleships are to bind by combat the quarg line forces. The cruisers are to hold their flanks and prevent the intrusion of enemy light forces into our order. Third Destroyer Division, simulate an attack on enemy aircraft carriers and prevent their orderly release of pursuit planes."

The commanders of the ships duplicated the Admiral's orders and detailed them within the limits of their authority.

When Captain Clarke completed the assignment of his subordinates, I drew his attention:

"Captain, Sir, your permission to send the carriers of the boarding drones together with the torpedo bombers. There are breaches in the armor of the enemy flagship, it's a good way in for my robots."

"Permission given. You don't submit directly to me, Lieutenant. Do your job without looking back at me. I have my own concerns."

"That's right, Captain, Sir," I answered according to the regulations, and switched to the channel of communication with my people, "Inga, get the dropships ready for takeoff and tell the technicians to be ready to launch our ten pursuit planes and drone carriers."

"Igor, do you want to go there?"

"Someone has to cover for our boarders. Clark's pilots won't do it, they have their own agenda, they're clearing the way for torpedo bombers ."

"Who's gonna control the drones on boarding?"

"You, Inga. You're gonna stay here and you're gonna rule over the boarding from the aircraft carrier. I taught you that, and you did a pretty good job. Then, on my signal, you drop everything and lead our platoon in the dropships to the quarg flagship. But not before I give you my orders, or it's a sure suicide. Do you understand?"

"What are we gonna do there with our dropships?"

"The drones are too few. They can't handle boarding such a ship alone. If I succeed, I will give the order. If not, then no. Without an order don't move from the aircraft carrier. You understand?"

"That's right, Commander," Inga answered gloomily and switched off.

***

The blackness of space was all over me. The tactical projection of the command machine gave a good idea of what was going on around. After all, I'm not an astronaut. Fighting and just flying in space is not my thing. Well, to be a passenger, why not? I would even really enjoy the fantastic views of galaxies and nebulae, the gloomy beauty of the asteroid belts and the frenzied flames of solar prominences. But being on a planet makes me feel more comfortable, and I'm still going to try to get back there as soon as possible.

The battle broke out with new energy. The arrival of the Fifth Strike Fleet changed the balance of power, and the quargs began regrouping again, abandoning frontal impact and forming flanking columns of heavy ships to surround the core of Admiral Nelson's fleet. Only their giant flagship didn't change course. Accompanied by several cruisers, it continued to attack the center, getting closer to the planet, and sort of aiming at the point where the dead fortress previously hung in low orbit.

I strongly suspected that the purpose of such a maneuver was to prevent Admiral Nelson from regrouping the heavy ships, that will allow the flanking groupings of the enemy to prepare themselves for simultaneous strike, which, by my reckoning, our fleet may not have survived. Apparently, the quargs had no doubt that their flagship would stand out the time needed under the fire of our heavy ships, so they behaved so brazenly.

We were closing in on enemy ships. A pursuit plane is fast and spinning. The carriers of the boarding drones were staying together, in a compact group. Their flight was now led by Inga with the task of taking these fragile ships to the shadow zone of the quargs' air-defense systems. It was still a long way away, though.

The first wave of pursuit planes from Windhoek collided with similar quarg machines in an attempt to clear a path for torpedo bombers . We and the enemy suffered roughly equal losses, but the quargs haven't had time to create a tight barrier to our planes, and if I understood correctly, they wouldn't be able to do it in time.

Realizing that aviation was not doing its job, the commander of the quargs sent one and a half dozen destroyers to the flagship. These relatively small ships were able to successfully combat the pursuit planes due to their high speed, rather powerful weapons and good maneuverability. However, all of this was achieved through weak protectability. A destroyer shouldn't be in a battlefield near a battleship or a cruiser. One lucky hit from a battleship, and it turns into a pile of junk flying along random vectors. Admiral Nelson had experience of such battles and did not miss his chance. The battleships of the Fifth Strike Fleet stopped for a minute the exchange of fire with the cruisers covering the enemy's flagship, and cleared the way for the pursuit planes literally with a pair of coordinated salvos.

However, several enemy pursuit planes managed to break through to the relatively slow torpedo bombers . Torpedo bombers could effectively maneuvre under heavy ship fire, but there was little chance of them escaping the attack of pursuit planes. My drone carriers, too, would surely have been through a lot, had the quargs known what was hidden beneath the hulls of those machines. And as it was, enemy pursuit planes paid little attention to a dozen obsolete machines that did not fire on them. Their primary target was the torpedo bombers , which they tackled first.

Having lost seven of their thirty wards, Wellington's pursuit planes pilots destroyed the quargs who managed to have burst. I don't know what Captain Clark told them on the command channel, I didn't have access to it, but I think the commanders of the flights and squadrons have heard a lot about themselves and their abilities.

However, we have approached the enemy's flagship and entered the area within the range of its cannons and direct defensive missiles. On the armored side of the enemy ship, there were more than enough anti-aircraft points. A swarm of small-calibre shells and homing rockets, which I had no fear of, flew at us. Our EW stations were superior to anything the quargs have encountered so far, so their scanners didn't see us very clearly, and the guidance systems were constantly losing target lock.

Taking into account that neither my pursuit planes nor the carriers of boarding drones were actively engaged in the battle, the quargs have completely switched to more active and visible targets, namely the pursuit planes from Windhoek and Wellington, and especially, torpedo bombers , which were the only ones, out of the attacking air wave, that they considered to be really dangerous to the large enemy ship.

I stopped watching the details of the fight. We were approaching the aft of the huge battleship I knew had hull damage. I was about to enter the game. The surviving torpedo bombers fired a coordinated salvo and began to reverse course. The battleship's air defense systems immediately lost interest in them and engaged in the twenty-five torpedoes heading for the ship's carcass. They failed to shoot them all down, and four binary rounds hit the armor. Only two of the torpedoes that exploded were able to break through. It certainly was unpleasant for the giant, but given its size, I don't think the ship was really badly damaged. But one of the gaps I thought was very promising for my purposes. The armored plates broke apart on the area of several tens of metres, allowing access to the interior of the ship, where the flow of fast-frozen gases took out all the rubbish, which formed when the high explosive component of the torpedo penetrated the armor.

"Inga, it's time!" I've marked the breach on the tactical projection and sent the data to the aircraft carrier. The drone carriers made a maneuver, sharply reducing the distance with the enemy's flagship. The battleship's air defense systems attempted to respond to the threat, but quickly switched to my pilotless pursuit planes, which had previously been passive, but now also took a 90-degree turn and flew towards the quarg ship, while firing all weapons and launching missiles at the flagship. The fact that this attack could not have done any harm to the battleship was not even secondary to me, it was not important at all. I needed to distract the enemy's air defense with my activity from the non-firing machines with the boarding drones on board. Active target always takes priority, and the wreckage of nine of my pursuit planes began to patter the thick armor of the quarg's flagship, but all ten carriers had been able to drop drones before the battleship's air defense tore them to shreds.

"Igor, the boarding drones have reached the hull of the enemy ship," I heard Inga's focused voice in my battle helmet, "I gave an order to get inside."

I turned into an extra. The boarding was now run by Inga. To get the drones off her, I had to be aboard the enemy battleship and to put on my specialized armor space suit from the Kapteen operation, the suit that my eggheads carefully upgraded every time they brought another development to mind. And now I've been forced to hang in my command plane not far from the huge enemy ship, hiding behind interference from EW stations and afraid to move so as not to attract the enemy's attention, because I was left alone. The pursuit planes left to escort home the torpedo bombers which have finished firing.

"Contact with enemy," Inga reported, "The drones encountered repair robots trying to repair the damage. Enemy destroyed. Moving on."

The battle in space continued in the meantime. I saw on the tactical projection, the markings of streamers faded from both sides, but ours, unfortunately, were extinguished more often. Another orbital fortress was destroyed by the fire of the monstrous guns of the quarg flagship, New York battleship has gone out of action, cruisers and destroyers were annihilated by dozens. The landing transports were staying far away from the battle, they were ready at any moment to either race off and jump out of the system, or send troops to the planets to support the planetary forces.

"I would really like to have you here, guys," I thought, looking at marks of ships of General Knyazev, but no landing transport can break through the battle dispositions of battleships and cruisers.

"Special drone-3 has located a special technical port," Inga's report took me away from my thoughts, "I authorized connection. The drone reported the successful launch of an adaptive network hacking algorithm."

Each carrier contained five boarding drones, and only four of them were equipped like full-fledged combat machines, the fifth drone was designed and built as a hacker of networks and control systems. I thought it would be foolish not to take advantage of the rich experience with the quarg's trophy weapons. The heavy ship, of course, is not the Small Dragon or the enemy dropship, but the general principles still remain, and the adaptive hacking algorithms extracted from my memory allowed to penetrate virtually every security system known here.

And now, a six-legged robot, small compared to even a Goanna, found with a scanner a technical port under the external plating of the corridor, robot quickly reached it with it's arms-manipulators, and connected to the ship's network.

"New contact with the enemy," Inga reported, "These were already live quargs. Crewmen in space suits came to see what was going on. The enemy was wiped out. There was no resistance. They didn't seem to have any weapons."

Boarding drones don't take prisoners. They only have two regimes: raid and capture. If we don't send drones to capture the ship, the drones aim to inflict maximum damage on all internal infrastructure, drones destroy the most important parts and assemblies and exterminate the crew. If a ship is to be captured, the crew becomes a priority target.

"There's access to the network!" - The triumph resonated in Inga's voice, "What do we do next, Commander? What are the orders to give the drone?"

I was frankly afraid to contact. EW stations - that's good, of course, but activity on the air... But there was nothing I could do. I configured a narrowly focused antenna, recorded my response, and sent it to Wellington in a compact packet.

"Inga, give him the task of intercepting the battleship's air-defense systems at least in my sector. I need to get into the ship myself, or there's nothing I can do."

"Doing it."

I was waiting. After all, the quargs detected my transmission. Of course it wasn't intercepted, but it was discovered. The EW system was alarmingly beeping, alerting me to the active scan from the battleship. The antiaircraft guns' barrels started moving. Apparently, they couldn't exactly capture the target, but they got the general direction right. If all the guns fire, I'll have to maneuver, which will reduce the effectiveness of the camouflage. The nearest antiaircraft gun released a burst of fire that went far away, but the quargs didn't calm down. The next few rounds were closer. Now at least ten weapons have fired. Another salvo fell so close, I clearly understood, the next turn is mine. I put the engine on a fast track and changed positions, but I couldn't seem to keep up. The gun barrels confidently followed me and... stood still.

"The air defense of the sector is under control," Inga reported cheerfully.

"Thank you, my dear," I said, not turning on the connection, "I'll give you a cookie the size of a battleship."

The breach in the hull was enough for my pursuit plane. I gently injected it into the breach and lowered it onto the disfigured deck. The high-explosive charge has done a great job, but gravity in a former hangar or warehouse, you can't tell by now, it's been sustained without a glitch.

I've never taken off and put on combat gear so fast. We were, of course, persecuted by this process tirelessly, but the combat situation, it's really stimulating.

"Inga, can you hear me?"

"More or less," the answer came from Wellington through the rustle and the squeaks. Still, the low-powered transponder system didn't work too well that far. But it still worked!

"Give me boarding control and wait for the signal. Get our guys up, let them sit in the dropships ready."

I completely turned my attention to controlling the boarding drones. Their cheerful advance into the interior of the ship has stalled. If the quargs had provided some antiboarding facilities for their battleship, our six-legged robots would have been shredded long ago, they were too few aboard such a ship. But there was no boarding, and the crews of the heavy ships had only light personal weapons. But the boarding hasn't been practiced here, and the crews of the heavy ships had only light personal weapons. However, the thick emergency bulkheads were perfectly capable of isolating the enemy without heavy weapons in the compartments he had captured. And the quargs would have done it, but instead of a heavy weapon, I had another mean, invisible weapon, which was now struggling to penetrate rather sophisticated security systems and sought access to control of the ship.

I plunged into the log files of the special drones and looked at what was available to me at the moment. Without proper supervision, the robots broke everything, down to sanitation systems. Of course, you could cause the enemy a lot of trouble by blocking the ship's restrooms, but in the current situation, it was not quite what I was aiming for. I've adjusted the efforts of my wards and added my combat equipment, which I once used to subdue the quarg dropship on Kapteen, to the capacities of five specialized hacking robots. The process went smoother, and about 15 minutes later, I called the aircraft carrier again.

"Inga, it's time! I've blocked the ship's self-destruct system. Now we can take it warm. How's the situation over there? Can you bring three of our dropships here? By your arrival, the battleship air-defence systems will be completely silent."

"It sucks, Commmander. The quargs scratched off two more fortresses and hit the flanks. Our battleships are on their last legs. Soon the enemy destroyers will reach the aircraft carriers. But we'll get there. The distance to you is much shorter, so wait for us to visit."

"I'm really looking forward to it. I'm kind of stuck here without you."

"I'm already in the hangar, we're on our way. All right. I'll see you later, Igor," Inga cut off the comms, and I went back into the process of intercepting the battleship. I was very disturbed by the crew. They saw what was happening to their networks and control units and actively tried to resist, by switching selected posts to manual control. But a sophisticated technical device like a giant battleship is simply impossible to operate manually, and we struggled, constantly swinging the situation around an invisible point of equilibrium.

Chapter 8

The flagship of the Fifth Strike Fleet, the newest battleship, Beijing, was still in service. Half of the main-caliber towers were silent, but the ship kept its course and maneuvrability. Survivalist systems managed the damage, albeit with difficulty. They have so far managed... In the ship's most secure facility, its command post, Admiral Nelson continued to direct the battle. He didn't give a damn about the forecast numbers the analysts gave.

"92% chance of victory of the enemy?" - asked the Admiral, "Shove those numbers up... I don't have time for you, though. Windhoek, how many attack planes do you have left? I need the 14th quarg streamer no longer pressure on the 5th Fortress, otherwise it won't last half an hour."

"Admiral, Sir," space control operator distracted the commander from combat control, "Quarg flagship fire has dropped 40 per cent. All of it's cannons appear intact, but many of his towers have stopped firing."

"Who's closest to him, let him report the situation. Study the question, then give me a resume."

"Yes, Sir."

***

For Inga's dropships, I've opened an external airlock for the technical hangar in the area under my control. The battleship's air defense was effectively blocked by my drones. It was a tough fight for space scanning systems, but I did manage to make it more difficult to find the dropships, which were already well camouflaged by the best in the world EW stations. It's a good thing there was a kind of emptiness around the quarg flagship. Having thrown it into the attack on our center, the quargs practically sacrificed the escort of their superbattleship. The flagship itself, in principle, withstood the fire of our heavy ships, but the cruisers, and especially the destroyers, were annihilated pretty quickly. In a large-scale battle like this, such a sacrifice is not uncommon, especially since the end justified the losses. And with their task of trapping the Fifth Strike Fleet, the quargs have done well, now Admiral Nelson was in so much trouble because of the powerful flank attack. Except the enemy's flagship ended up alone.

Dropships have descended on the hangar deck, and the heavy steps of the assault drones that produced vibrations of the floorboards, but were silent in a vacuum, heralded the arrival of Inga's platoon. The second drone squad was run by Fulton and the third by Jaswinder. I chose to take with me comrades tested in battle, and as it turned out, not for nothing.

The guns of the small boarders were no match for the weapons of the assault drones. In designing boarding robots, I used the minimum sizes, so that they can fit into any slit, technical well or ventilation shaft, but I never expected them to take control of such a giant, that even had internal emergency bulkheads almost as thick as the destroyer's side.

But now things went smoothly. I managed to lift some of the bulkheads by taking the reins of their controls, but many of them were manually blocked, making this approach impossible. On the other hand, anti-tank missiles turned out to be good picklocks. Well, if not from the first try, then from the third...

So, we were moving forward, and every new communication hub, that we managed to capture, gave me new opportunities to penetrate the battleship control system more and more.

***

The fifth orbital fortress could not be saved. A desperate attack by eight torpedo bombers covered by the remnants of the pursuit planes wing of the aircraft carrier Windhoek caused heavy damage to the enemy battleship, but the ship that came out of the battle was replaced by three cruisers, that crushed the fifth orbital fortress by coordinated salvos in 40 minutes. Now the only dilapidated fortress remained over the entire southern hemisphere of Barnard-3, around it the remnants of the Fifth Strike Fleet and several surviving ships of the Tenth and Twelfth fleets closed the ranks.

"Admiral, Sir, the enemy flagship has stopped firing. It continues to approach the planet, but does not maneuver or fire," reported the operator.

"Analysts, what's going on? Or can you only count the odds of us being defeated?" Nelson snapped.

"We have information from Wellington aircraft carrier," the senior analyst responded in a hurry, "At the beginning of the battle, it's aircraft group accompanied torpedo bombers in an attack on the enemy flagship. Lieutenant Lavroff joined the attackers with his experimental machines. Then, about an hour ago, apparently on Lavroff's orders, his platoon of commandos left the aircraft carrier on three dropships. Throughout the battle, Lieutenant Lavroff maintained contact with his subordinates aboard Wellington. That's all I could find out."

"Lavroff... again Lavroff," the Admiral was grinning rapaciously, "everywhere he appears, there's something strange going on. Let's see what happens this time... Fffuck! Clark! What's going on?"

"Attacked by enemy destroyers, Admiral, fighting!" shouted back the aircraft carrier Wellington's commander.

"Retreat immediately! Cruiser Moscow! Abandon formation and cover Captain Clark's retreat!"

***

A large ship always has a large crew, usually with excellent knowledge of its vessel. The quargs were not cowards and, despite being completely unprepared for such a turn of events, they resisted, making barricades and obstructions, and even leaving in the corridors improvised mines made of anti-aircraft shells. Naturally, we couldn't be stopped by all this amateur actions, but we were wasting time, and in space, beyond the thick sides of the enemy ship, in those lost moments our comrades were dieing.

But something has been done. I haven't been able to intercept the main weapons yet, but the enemy has already lost control of them. At some point, it became clear to me that I could not take full control of the ship without access to the command post. Again, it was a manifestation of the rigid vertical subordination so characteristic of the society of our adversaries. No quarg could have imagined that command of the ship could be taken from somewhere other than the command post, and the whole battleship control system was rigged to do just that. Many commands from other locations did not go through just physically, on a hardware level.

At the entrance to the command level, the quargs must have collected everything they could have prepared in the short time they had at their disposal. The wide trunk corridor was blocked by a barricade made of some hastily dismantled heavy equipment, and behind it... there was an anti-aircraft gun, probably dragged from the back-up depot, maybe taken off the side, the quargs could really do even that.

Two of the assault drones who were the first to enter this level, were torn to pieces by the volley of the anti-aircraft gun. That was a really mighty cannon. But it was a desperate gesture. What can fighters do in ordinary, unarmored space suits, even if they have a serious gun? They can only die heroically. The quargs succeeded. They've earned my respect. I think the enemies were slightly contorted by the sound of their own gunshots in a confined space, and after an anti-tank missile flew into the corridor and exploded somewhere near the barricade, the quargs lost their fighting power. In any case, our three assault drones that broke into the level after the missile exploded only got a poorly aimed volley, that demolished the ceiling and the wall, and then it was over in seconds.

That's it. Now the ship is definitely ours.

***

Nelson looked gloomily at the projection screen. He watched the last orbital fortress, that had covered the southern hemisphere of the planet, now it was descending from orbit and falling apart, and its pieces were burning in the dense atmosphere of Barnard-3. Even this Iron Admiral seemed no longer able to look at the death of his fleet, or perhaps the beginning of the end of his civilization.

The balance of power was dismal. The quargs had 14 battleships, eight cruisers, three aircraft carriers and about five dozen smaller ships. Somewhere in the distance behind these ships, there was a formidable fleet of landing transports ready to attack the planets as soon as the fleet cleared their way to the surface. Of course, almost all of these ships were heavily damaged, but all of them were in varying degrees operational. And it was not at all clear what was happening to their flagship, drifting silently towards the planet.

Nelson had three heavily beaten battleships, of which only his Beijing still represented some real power. Nine cruisers with varying degrees of damage were, of course, still quite capable of fighting, but not against the battleships that outnumbered them. The aircraft carrier Wellington, damaged after the destroyer attack, hid behind the backs of the line forces together with his fellow Windhoek under the protection of two dozen destroyers and corvettes.

And the quargs were slowly regrouping, clearly hoping to end the fleet of humans with a final decisive strike, and they had every reason to do that.

The Admiral was faced with a difficult choice. He could fight without a chance to win, or could retreat to the other side of the planet where three orbital fortresses still existed, but it meant opening the way for the quargs landing forces to the densely populated Barnard-3.

The Admiral had no idea that, in fact, he was trying to solve the same enigma that Lieutenant Lavroff had already met once, but Nelson's was luckier, he didn't have to make that decision.

"The call from the quarg flagship!" That was a surprised exclamation from the communications operator.

"Turn it on."

On the projection screen appeared a three-dimensional image of a room filled with unfamiliar equipment of unusual design. Lieutenant Lavroff, in a heavy infantry combat suit with the visor of his helmet lifted up, was standing behind some kind of space control console. The barrels of the automatic gun and the rotary machine-gun sticking behind his shoulders, looked strange at the command post of the spaceship, as well as the light combat robot Goanna, trampling in the hallway behind the Lieutenant's back, which apparently couldn't walk through the door.

"Admiral, Sir," Lavroff told Nelson, "Enemy flagship is under our control. Please indicate the location in the combat order and the mission."

Nelson was silent. This boy has done the impossible for the Earth Federation again.

"Admiral, Sir, the quarg ships are in motion," space control operator interrupted the pause.

"How much control do you have over the ship, Lieutenant?"

"I can do simple maneuvers, fire all the main-calibre weapons, and if necessary, rocket and torpedo weapons, Admiral, Sir. Air defence systems are now fully automated. Overall, combat damage is not critical, but the ship should not be attacked by torpedo bombers."

"Take the coordinates of your position in formation. You are to command the ship... What would you call the ship, Lieutenant?"

"Titan, Admiral, Sir," answered the commando after some thought, "This is where I was born and raised."

"Well, Lieutenant Lavroff, that name fits YOUR ship perfectly."

***

When I turned on the marching engines and clumsily took a place in the battle formation of the remnants of the Fifth Strike Fleet, there was confusion among the quargs. For a few minutes, their ships were moving without any system, and then feverishly lined up into battle order and attacked. There was no trace of their slowness or serenity left.

I checked the ammo for the main guns, and hemmed with satisfaction. There were still enough shells. The admiral's orders were to concentrate all fire on the enemy's least damaged battleship, and as soon as the crazy, as far as I'm concerned, guided navigation system of my battship captured the target, I ordered the main-caliber towers to open fire.

The distance was still too great, and the accuracy of the shooting left much to be desired, but I still got two hits. Of course, the battleship is not a destroyer, and even a heavy projectile like mine couldn't have blown it to shreds on one hit. The enemy ship shook, swerved from the course, but did not lose its speed and did not come out of the battle. I was the only one who's fired from our fleet so far. For the rest of the ships, the distance to the targets still exceeded the capability of their cannons.

The quargs were completely changed. Instead of an aggressive yet calculating and intelligent enemy, a furious beast appeared before us, who threw himself at the enemy without regard to anything. The capture of their mighty flagship by humans meant something very important to the enemy, and the quargs were willing to pay any price for not to leave this unique ship in enemy hands.

The enemy attacked in their classic formation. In the front were battleships and the least damaged cruisers, which lined up in some kind of disc. In the second echelon came smaller ships or with more serious damage, and even further, the aircraft carriers were guarded by destroyers and corvettes. Admiral Nelson's ships have not been fired upon. The quarg's entire fire was focused on my battleship, and despite my not-so-elegant maneuvering attempts, Titan was constantly shuddered by heavy shells. Not all of them penetrated the armor, and the ones that did, they were destroying not the most vital compartments adjacent to the hull. However, these attacks disabled an increasing number of short-range anti-aircraft guns and missile and torpedo shafts. My ship became increasingly vulnerable in close combat, and I became more and more aware that it was wrong to let the quargs near it.

"Admiral, Sir," I told Nelson, "Request permission to fire on enemy aircraft carriers. Distance allows, and if they let out the air force and get to Titan, I'll have practically nothing to meet them."

"Twenty percent of the main-calibre weapons can be used to combat aircraft carriers. With the rest of them, continue to suppress the enemy's battleships," answered the Admiral almost at once, "The 2nd Destroyer Division to secure Titan battleship from a possible air attack."

That decision was highly controversial, I remembered what happened to the quarg destroyers that tried to stop our pursuit planes under heavy ship fire, but now the quargs seemed blind. They saw nothing but their former flagship, and Nelson took a risk.

The distance to the enemy was being reduced. Nelson's battleships, which were not fired upon by the enemy, fired like in a shooting range without even maneuvring. The enemy's streamers were extinguished on tactical projection one by one, but my battleship has been increasingly beaten. Out of ten huge main-caliber towers, seven remained in service. Multiple hits to already fractured plating areas resulted in increasingly critical damage, and despite the repeated duplication of the most important units and mechanisms, the battleship was getting worse and worse. I have stopped the maneuvring attempts because at such a distance they no longer reduced the effectiveness of enemy fire.

I burned one of the enemy aircraft carriers after all. I don't know where my shell went, but the quarg ship was swollen from the inside out like a bright star, which in a second turned into a cloud of faintly luminous gas and dust, and it quickly dissipated in the vacuum of space. However, two other aircraft carriers managed to release torpedo bombers and pursuit planes despite the damage they sustained. From that moment on, aircraft carriers were no longer of interest to me, and without waiting for the order, I directed the cannons that fired on them back to the enemy's heavy ships. However, the quargs had practically no more battleships, with the exception of the ruins of three ships more or less still in their original shape, they kept flying in our direction like unguided metal piles and occasionally flashed by the few surviving guns.

The surviving ships of the Fifth Strike Fleet were already capable of handling the remaining quarg forces, but now I wasn't worried about the big enemy streamers, I was worried about the torpedo bombers . There were surprisingly many of them. Either the quargs kept these machines in reserve, or they just haven't found their use in this battle until now, but there was now a wave of 55 torpedo bombers approaching Titan, covered by hundred pursuit planes. I had strong doubts that a division of ten destroyers assigned to me should be able to defeat them.

Admiral Nelson also understood it.

"Captain Lavroff, reversal of previous targets. Set barrage fire against enemy aircraft. Main calibre."

It was an act of desperation. The main caliber wasn't meant to fight the mosquito fleet. Of course, when there are really many cannons, as I have now, there will surely be some effect, but against the pursuit planes and torpedo bombers, it's still completely useless.

"Admiral, Sir," it was not my idea of fun to stand still and wait for the beating to start, "Allow evasive maneuvre towards northern hemisphere of Barnard-3. There are still three orbital fortresses. If I can get behind them in time, the quarg aircraft will be given warm welcomes. With a high probability, all the enemy's streamers will follow me, and you'll be able to provide flanking fire on them."

In a standard situation, my offer seemed risky, but Nelson saw perfectly well that the quargs were clutching at my

Titan with a stranglehold, and ignore all the other targets, so he decided to take the risk.

"Permission given," replied the Admiral, "Second Destroyer Division to follow Titan and provide cover from enemy torpedo bombers ."

The engines of the battleship were intact, and even though the power plant was producing only seventy percent of the power, the maneuver was quite sharp. After all, the quargs equipped their new ship with all the best of the latest developments, and it felt that way. Of course, the battleship couldn't compete in the acceleration with pursuit planes and torpedo bombers, but I couldn't but take that chance. Although, to be honest, the odds looked pretty doubtful. By all accounts, I didn't make it. I understood it, and so did the quargs. So they pursued the former flagship of their fleet, trying to escape, with even more heat. However, I, who was Brigadier General Dean, did not love space for nothing, I preferred planets to space, yet they are closer to me. I didn't go round Barnard-3 along a wide arc, I sent a giant ship into the atmosphere.

"Lieutenant Lavroff, what are you doing?" I heard Nelson screaming on the communications channel.

"Taking evasive action as planned, Admiral, Sir," I said, brazenly per se, but politely in form, sensing the hull trembling, as I'm used to being a commando, as the ship entered the upper atmosphere, "Let the enemy enter low orbits. Down there, anti-orbital missiles in the mines and Bisons of planetary forces are impatiently waiting for his ships."

"You're an adventurer, Captain Lavroff! I already doubt my decision to entrust you with a ship," stated Admiral Nelson, but I didn't hear much condemnation in his voice, and the order 'to stop the outrage' did not follow as well.

Titan was shaking and rocking. From the surface, a giant battleship bursting the atmosphere must have looked fabulous. I was even jealous of the potential audience for the play I performed. The speed plummeted and the enemy began to shorten the distance even faster than at the beginning of my maneuver. But now the whole situation looked completely different. The enemy could attack me from only one side - the outer space. I was leading the ship almost along the edge of the atmosphere, only slightly plunging into it, but in doing so, I've diverted the most damaged side of the battleship to the planet, and it was protecting me from the most vulnerable side. The destroyers that escorted Titan did not enter the atmosphere, but they, too, were relieved by the narrowing of the field of possible attack vectors.

Planetary forces from the surface have already been sending me requests for target designation for their missile guidance systems, and I was delighted to transmit the scanner data. As a result, when the first wave of quargs reached the torpedo launch range, many hundreds of anti-orbital missiles have already flown towards them from the planet. Since my last battle in a previous life, I have not seen such a powerful ground-based anti-space defence salvo, but then it was the toads that gave us such a bad time. Now I could only rejoice in the density of fire. Ground forces that sat idle on the planet during the space battle, seemed to be just happy to be able to finally contribute to this now imminent victory, and they did a great job. Even the atmospheric air force, acting at its maximum altitude, was trying to cover my battleship. Whole squadrons of pursuit planes were rushing a few kilometers under Titan, trying to reach the enemy with their missiles. The real effectiveness of this shooting was around zero, but at least they stopped the enemy pursuit planes and torpedo bombers from providing precision fire.

And yet the quargs were able to fight well, even being kind of fiercely blinded because of their flagship's seizure. The Titan's hulk was struck by fifteen torpedoes. Even for a giant like that, it was a lot. The power plant was down to 40 percent, less than half of the main-calibre cannons survived, and the pieces of armor began to fall off the damaged parts of the hull under the influence of the atmosphere. I realized that the battleship could not survive beyond this mode of motion, and by a neat maneuver brought it back into space.

While I was trying to escape and retracted the quargs, Admiral Nelson did not waste any time. Taking advantage of the favourable conditions of the battle, his ships were comfortably shooting the remains of the quarg fleet, and by the time I got to the area of responsibility of one of the planet's northern hemisphere orbital fortresses, they had no one to fight.

The quarg warships were gone, and the fleet of landing transports, which remained idle during the battle, picked up speed and jumped out of the system.

The last pursuit planes and torpedo bombers were in a desperate position. They couldn't reach Titan beyond the orbital fortresses anymore, and there weren't many left, and they had nowhere to return, their aircraft carriers died fighting Admiral Nelson's ships. However, the quargs did not surrender and perished, all of them, in a suicide attack on the orbital fortress that covered my ship.

"Admiral, Sir, evasive maneuvre completed. The ship's fighting capability is 35%," I reported to Nelson."Asking for further guidance."

"Congratulations on your victory, gentlemen!" - declared the Admiral over the public channel, disregarding my report, "It's been given to us at a high price. Too high. But it's still a win. Ship commanders, within one hour, report casualties and damage and arrange for the evacuation of the wounded to planetary hospitals."

I was waiting for the Admiral's order. I didn't see the point in being on Titan for too long. Yes, I am formally appointed commander of this huge ship, but that doesn't change the fact that I was an accidental man here with no connection to the Fleet. Of course, I'm the only one who could control a giant battleship, so the Admiral had to make a difficult decision about what to do with me and my trophy. After two hours, Nelson made a decision.

"Lieutenant Lavroff," he called me on a closed channel, "you report that the ship's running systems are normal. Can you do a series of jumps to get to Earth?"

"That's right, Admiral, Sir. Technically, I can do that, but my knowledge of hyperspace navigation is grossly inadequate. I'll need a specialist on board."

"I'll send you an interim team, Lieutenant. Navigator officers will be in it, too. It would be also nice to clean up your ship. Enemy bodies in the pods are not conducive to their habitability. Three destroyers and aircraft carriers, Wellington and Windhoek, will accompany you, anyway, they're useless without pursuit planes and torpedo bombers. Admiral Fulton has been appointed commander of the crossing. He's going on Windhoek."

***

In the Solar System, we were met by destroyers of the Metropolitan fleet and escorted to the Martian shipyards. My Titan, of course, couldn't go in any docks, but there was no attempt to place it.

General of the Army Barrington contacted me, and, to my surprise, asked me strange questions.

"Mr Lavroff," he got to the point after he congratulated me on my victory, "How do you plan to dispose of your grand trophy?"

"General of the Army, Sir," I took the liberty of adding a note of surprise to my voice, "And how can I dispose of it, except to hand it over to the Fleet's moppers-up?"

"Ehh...Mr Lavroff, so you haven't spoken to your lawyers yet? Well, I understand you've just come from fighting and crossing, but, okay, I'll explain the situation to you myself. The thing is, you didn't get on board the Wellington air carrier by order of your superiors, but, so to speak, on your own initiative, and not on the initiative of Lieutenant Lavroff, who would grant such a request from a mere Lieutenant commando? Now, you and your men boarded a Fifth Strike Fleet ship as part of the agreement to test new equipment, and acted not as soldiers and officers of the Federation Army, but as the head of the Lavroff Weapons Company and the specialists he brought. All your equipment belonged to your private company, and not to the Army or the Fleet. You weren't even supposed to be in combat, since the agreement did not provide for combat tests, but for preliminary tests. But the quargs' attack on Barnard's star system had confused all plans. As a result, again, on your own initiative, you joined the air carrier attack, aimed at the enemy flagship, which you eventually captured, and then willingly joined the forces of the Fifth Strike Fleet under the command of Admiral Nelson."

I listened to General Barrington, and I spent more and more energy holding my jaw still, for it was rapidly growing heavier and threatened to fall to the floor every second of the day. But I held on. The General, meanwhile, continued:

"As a result, the following picture emerges: The head and employees of the Lavroff Weaponry Company during the battle at Barnard-3, using their own equipment and weapons, captured the newest enemy ship, and with its help personally destroyed four battleships and the aircraft carrier of the enemy. In addition, along with the ships of the Fifth Strike Fleet, you participated in the destruction of ten more enemy battleships and and a significant number of streamers of the class below. Your actions ensured the victory of the Federation Fleet in a major battle and prevented the capture of a densely populated planet by the enemy.

By the way, I can congratulate you, Mr Lavroff, you will be given this information officially, but you and your people have been honorary citizens of the planet Lantan for a week. That's Barnard-3's own name."

"Serving the Earth Federation," I answered with a wooden voice, continuing the struggle with my jaw.

"Now, what this implies is the following. Mr Lavroff, the enemy ship you have captured, by all legal grounds, is the property of the Lavroff Weapons Company, of which you are the head. Moreover, all expenses incurred by your company during the battle of Barnard-3, the Ministry of Defense is obliged to reimburse you, and I assure you, it will do so with great pleasure, 'cause if it hadn't been for your involvement in the battle, our losses in equipment, people and resources would have been calculated in such numbers, in comparison with which this reimbursement looks like the cost of a first-grader's breakfast at school."

"But..."

"Wait, Mr Lavroff, I haven't told you everything yet. For the destruction of five enemy first-rate ships and active participation in the destruction of an entire list of the enemy streamers, your company is entitled to a bonus, the amount of which is still being calculated, but rest assured that this bonus will exceed the above-mentioned compensation for your expenses several times."

I was thinking feverishly. I needed the money, but I didn't fight for it. On the other hand, it's foolish to refuse, because I'm still going to spend that money developing new weapons for the Army and the Fleet. In Barrington's mood, I saw very well that he understood that too and that he was only happy to give me these funds, hoping to get even better weapons in exchange for them.

"I repeat my question, Mr Lavroff. What do you plan to do with Titan battleship?"

"It would depend on the needs of the Fleet, General of the Army, Sir," I replied, having given some thought to the question, "if it needs such a ship, the Lavroff Weapons Company is ready to repair and re-equip Titan on the order of the Ministry of Defense, and after that, to hand it over to the Fleet."

"To hand it over?" the General grinned, "You're forgetting the status of your trophy again. Not to hand it over, but to sell! Incidentally, the combat damage sustained by your battleship is also part of your expenses, 'cause when you took it into battle, it had already been owned by your company. Accordingly, 80% of the repairs will be funded by the Ministry of Defence. And, yes. The Fleet is very interested in buying your trophy. It will be fully studied and not only put into operation under the flag of the Federation, but also serve as a prototype for the construction of our own ships of this class."

Epilogue

The President extended to me an invitation to a private reception at his country residence. A beautiful, spacious park with landscaped presidential palace structures made a pleasant impression on me. On the occasion of wonderful sunny weather our meeting took place in an open pavilion. I couldn't believe this place was once covered in ice a few kilometers thick.

"Mr Lavroff," the Commander-in-Chief of the Earth Federation Armed Forces smiled at me, "I'm glad to see you again."

"So am I, Mr President," I responded, shaking the hand of the Head of State and accepting his style of addressing me without mentioning military rank.

"Your last operation left a deep impression on all of us," said Tobolsky in low voice, "Let's have a seat at the table. We're having tea with my favorite ginger cookies. We have a lot to talk about, Mr Lavroff."

I followed the only Marshal in the Earth Federation Army in silence. The cookies were really tasty, and the high-mountain grasses tea was unexpectedly pleasant.

"Thyme, Rhododendron and Hawthorn Flowers," explained the President, satisfied with my countenance after the first sip, "plus some Marjoram and shelf fungus. It's delicious, it's healthy, and it's a good tonic."

I was delighted to have tea and listen to the Head of State, who was in no hurry to have a serious conversation. The President hasn't been sleeping much, and he's been very tired lately. It was noticeable, and I kept the small talk, not preventing Tobolsky from relaxing a little before a serious conversation.

"Mr Lavroff," the President finally got down to business, "In the last year, you've done more for the Earth Federation than anyone else. You are an officer who is not afraid of risk and finds a way out of situations that seem hopeless. And you're the owner of a private company, but both I, and all of my entourage, we clearly see that profit is secondary to you and is important only to the extent that it contributes to your goals. What do you seek, Mr Lavroff?"

"A while ago," I smiled a little, "I was asked a similar question. This was on Ganymede when I was applying to the Planetary Commando Academy. So I told the Colonel who chaired the commission that I wanted to see our victory for myself and to lead a landing party to the mother planet of the quargs. Things have changed since then. I'm older and my appetites have grown. I don't just want to win this war, Mr President. I want to make sure that the Earth Federation is able not only to defeat the quargs, but also to win future, more terrible conflicts."

Tobolsky certainly did not expect such a statement. He looked at me in surprise and asked:

"Do you think there's anything more frightening than the invasion of the quargs?"

"I'm sure of it, Mr President. I can't give you a precise time frame, but after victory, our expansion will not stop, which means we will move deeper and deeper into unexplored space. We've already met strangers. And these were aliens armed to the teeth, mind you. And we were very weak back then. We were not prepared to face such an enemy, and for some reason the enemy was ready. Why do you think that is? Because our meeting was as much of a surprise to the quargs as it was to us."

"You speak of our victory as a fait accompli..."

"We'll make it a fact, Mr President, otherwise there's no point in discussing anything else."

"Your confidence is contagious, Mr Lavroff... So you believe that prior to meeting us, the quargs faced someone else in the war?"

"I'm pretty sure, Mr President. And I'm also seriously concerned that the quargs invaded us not just because we were standing in the way of their expansion. Someone is pushing them out of the previously developed territories or they live under the constant threat of an attack by a stronger enemy. I have no solid evidence of this hypothesis, but we cannot ignore this possibility and must be prepared for any development."

The President has been thinking for a long time. All the accumulated fatigue and strain of recent months have now been reflected on his face.

"You haven't seen a life of peace, Mr Lavroff," suddenly the President changed the subject,"You were born and raised in a war. You don't know that life can be very different. And I remember that. I hate war, Mr. Lavroff. I hate it, you understand? And you've just told me that defeating the quargs is not the end yet, but probably the beginning of another great war..."

Probably, I understood Tobolsky. He didn't even know how right he was, saying I haven't seen a world without fighting and dying. In my first life, I was too late to be born to find peace. When I was born, the war had been going on for decades. I grew up in an orphanage, then I became cadet, officer, and finally brigadier general, and cadet and officer again. I didn't know how people lived without war, and Tobolsky knew, and he seemed to miss it a lot. So he had something to be sorry about. I was anxious to see a world without war, too. Probably the first time in my life I've ever wanted this so badly.

"Mr President, the opportunity to live in peace is worth the sacrifices and losses we are now suffering. I haven't really seen a peaceful life, but I remember an ancient rule: If you want peace, prepare for war. And I'm going to be well prepared."

Tobolsky looked silently at the green hills around for a while, then looked me in the eye.

"What do you need, Mr Lavroff, to advance our victory?"

I expected anything, but not this abstract question. But I was well aware that in speaking to the President, one should not miss the opportunity. Well, Commander-in-Chief, I didn't twist your arm...

"The job of Minister of Military Production and unlimited budgetary funding."

The president flinched and looked at me with a new stare.

"You're not even 18 yet, Mr Lavroff. Are you sure you can afford such a post and such responsibility?"

"I think if you hadn't been convinced from the start, you wouldn't have asked me the previous question, Mr President."

"You're a very serious and purposeful man, Mr Lavroff, and I can see that there are concrete cases behind your confidence. The Lavroff Weapons Company has proved itself in the execution of state orders, but the Minister of Military Production is more of a political figure, and you haven't gained the necessary weight in this area yet. But I think you understand. I won't appoint you Minister, but I have another position for you, which will be no worse for your purposes, and in my opinion, even better. General Barrington, as he did at the beginning of the war, has once again been appointed by me as head of the Federation Rear Service, and his current post became vacant. This will be the first time in history that an officer with the rank of captain has been appointed to this job," Tobolsky grinned. "Don't act surprised, Mr Lavroff. For the defensive operation in the Barnard star system, you are represented by Admiral Nelson to the Order of Ushakov and to the extraordinary military rank. True, the Admiral acted within his authority and presented you to the rank of Senior Lieutenant, but Marshal Tobolsky has a few more options. So congratulations, Mr Lavroff, on your promotion to the rank of captain and on your new position. My decree appointing you head of the New Equipment and Weapons Commission of the Ministry of Defense will be ready within 24 hours."

"Serving the Earth Federation," I replied, rising up.

The President, too, rose up, making it clear that the meeting was over.

"Mr President, may I make a small request?"

"I'm listening," The Commander-in-Chief's voice expressed interest.

"I'm a combat officer, Mr President, and I'd like to stay that way. I request your permission to personally conduct tests and combat operations with the participation of adopted new military equipment, if needed."

"Why am I not surprised?" - Tobolsky grinned again.

To be continued.
Brigadier General. Book three. Assault Line.

Made in the USA
Monee, IL
10 February 2022